"I'm cur... ... t H.H.M. stands for..."

Her heart missed another beat, but recognizing he wouldn't let the matter drop, she decided on bluntness. "It stands for His High and Mightiness."

Without expression he regarded her. "You find me autocratic?"

"Very."

"Will it be a problem for you?"

"I give of my best if I'm not on the defensive."

"I had the impression you enjoyed a battle, Miss Stewart."

"I do—if it's a fair one."

ROBERTA LEIGH wrote her first book at the age of nineteen and since then has written more than seventy romance novels, as well as many books and film series for children. She has also been an editor of a woman's magazine and produced a teen magazine, but writing romance fiction remains one of her greatest joys. She lives in Hampstead, London, and has one son.

ROBERTA LEIGH

Two-Timing Man

Harlequin Books

TORONTO • NEW YORK • LONDON
AMSTERDAM • PARIS • SYDNEY • HAMBURG
STOCKHOLM • ATHENS • TOKYO • MILAN
MADRID • WARSAW • BUDAPEST • AUCKLAND

ISBN 0-373-11609-8

TWO-TIMING MAN

Copyright © 1993 by Roberta Leigh.

CHAPTER ONE

ARTHUR STEWART strode into his daughter's office as she was putting on her navy wool jacket. 'I'd like a word with you, Abby.'

'I'm on my way out, Dad. Can it wait?'

'I only wanted to tell you Henry Smallwood telephoned to say he liked the proposal we sent to him and is giving us the contract.'

'Fantastic!' Abby's green eyes sparkled with delight.

'All thanks to you, my girl. You put in a colossal amount of research, and the proposals you came up with were first class.'

'I enjoyed scouting around his stores asking questions.'

'And using those big eyes of yours to get honest answers! That's where we scored over our rivals. You did a marvellous presentation.'

'Thanks. When do I have another raise?'

Her father chuckled, knowing her question was rhetorical. 'The one thing Smallwood didn't like was the idea of building up the image of his top executives. He's a conservative man and thinks publicity should be given only to the stores.'

'We can do that too. But the managers and——'

'You don't have to persuade *me*, my dear,' Arthur Stewart cut in. 'Smallwood's the one. He wants to set up a meeting to discuss it.'

'Good,' Abby said. 'I'm sure I can change his mind.'

'Remember he's the old-fashioned type.'

'Meaning?'

'You'd be eye-catching if you wore a sack, so don't dress as if you've stepped out of *Vogue*!'

'Point taken.' She glanced at her watch. 'I really have to go. May we chew the fat later?'

'Sure. Where are you off to in such a hurry?'

'Caroline's.'

Her father didn't hide his surprise at the mention of his niece. 'I wasn't aware the two of you still kept in touch.'

'We don't. But she called this morning and asked me to go over. It sounded urgent.'

'Give her my love and tell her it's time we saw her and the baby again. He's the only great-nephew your mother and I have, and I can't understand why she keeps so damned distant.'

'Pride, I think. She made a fool of herself and she's ashamed of it.'

Arthur Stewart grunted. 'I still can't understand her marrying that good-for-nothing. As soon as I saw him I knew he was trouble, but she wouldn't hear a word against him.'

Driving across London, Abby couldn't help smiling at her father's old-fashioned description of Jeffrey Norton—though it was accurate enough. Handsome and loaded with charm, he had swept her nineteen-year-old cousin off her feet, and no amount of dissuasion from Abby's parents, who had adopted her after her own parents had been killed in a train crash when she was ten, could change her mind.

They had gone to live in Edinburgh, and for the first year her letters were ecstatic, especially when she had announced she was expecting a baby. But regular letters had gradually turned into brief, spasmodic cards, and after a few months had ceased altogether.

Then unexpectedly she had telephoned to say she had a baby son, and that Jeffrey had left her, withdrawing from their joint bank account most of the money she had inherited from her parents. Horrified, the Stewarts had immediately offered financial assistance, while Abby had volunteered to fly up and stay with her for a couple of weeks. But Caroline had refused all support, saying she was going to return to London and would let them know when she was coming.

There had been no further word from her, and when they tried to contact her they learned she had moved and left no forwarding address. It wasn't until months had passed that she called to say she was living in south London, had found a well-paid part-time job, and her landlady was acting as a baby-minder. She had also promised to bring the baby to see them.

It was a promise she had kept, and, though her aunt and uncle had been dismayed by her thinness and obvious unhappiness, she had still refused any assistance, insisting she was managing very well.

She had not visited them since, and her call to Abby today—asking to see her urgently—had come as a total surprise. It had meant cancelling an appointment with a client, but there was no way Abby could ignore the plea she had sensed in her cousin's voice, and she dreaded what she would find at the end of her journey.

The dread increased as she reached the address she had been given, and found it be a dilapidated, narrow-fronted Victorian house in a dingy street close to a gasworks.

Pressing the bell which bore her cousin's name, she pushed open the shabby front door and climbed three long flights to the top floor apartment where Caroline was waiting to greet her. Abby hugged her close, dismayed by her appearance; where before she had been pale and slender, she was now ashen and gaunt, and her hair, once almost identical to Abby's red-gold, was now pale and lustreless.

Apart from their hair-colouring and height—they were both five feet seven—there was little family resemblance between them. Her cousin's looks were chocolate-box perfect, whereas Abby's slightly irregular features stopped her from being conventionally beautiful. Yet she was the more arresting because of it: her nose tip-tilted with a sprinkling of freckles on the bridge, her mouth generously wide with a softly curving lower lip, her chin small but determined. High cheekbones enhanced green eyes fringed by thick lashes several shades darker than her hair, and her skin had a pearly translucence that several besotted men had likened to 'the dawn sky touched by the rising sun'.

'It's wonderful to see you,' she said now. 'Where's the infant?'

'Sleeping, thank goodness.' Caroline led the way into a small, sparsely furnished sitting-room. 'He has a terrible cold and I was up half the night with him. I won't take you in to him in case it wakes him.'

'Poor lamb,' Abby sympathised. 'I'll see him next time. But tell me how *you* are.'

'Let's have a cup of tea first.'

Abby's heart sank as she watched her cousin go across to a tiny sink unit in the corner and switch on an electric kettle. Gone was the happy smile and confident step of the beautiful girl of three years ago. In her place was a nervous wraith with deep shadows under her eyes and a smile that didn't go beyond her mouth. The room seemed to reflect her unhappiness, with its cheap furniture, worn carpet and tatty curtains, and Abby knew Caroline must be desperate for help to allow any member of her family to visit her here.

She was busy wondering what it might be, when a mug of tea was pushed into her hand and Caroline settled beside her on the rickety couch.

'I suppose you're dying to know why I wanted to see you,' the younger girl echoed her thoughts. 'It's nothing serious—just very awkward, and I'd no one else to turn to. But Mrs Wilson, my landlady who usually looks after Charlie, has flu, and I need someone to stay with him tonight.'

Abby couldn't believe her ears. 'You mean you want to go out and leave your baby when he isn't well?'

'Of course not! But I have no choice. If I stay at home I'll lose my job.'

'Your *job*?'

'Why else did you think I wanted you to help me? So I could go on a date?' Caroline's large brown eyes filled with tears, clear indication how perilous was her self-control.

Sympathetically Abby caught her hand. 'Surely your employer would understand.'

'He isn't the understanding sort. He'd fire me.'

'For not going in one night? What exactly do you do there?'

Her cousin stared at the carpet, then lifted her head defiantly. 'I'm a kitten at the Kitty Club.'

'You're *what*?'

'It isn't as bad as it sounds.'

'Who are you kidding? I went there once with a client and it was disgusting. All those leering men—how *could* you, Caro?'

'I had no choice. It pays better than any day job I could do, and I need the money.'

'You told us Jeffrey was supporting you,' Abby said angrily.

'OK, so I lied. I was ashamed to admit what a fool he had made of me. But I thought I could manage. And I *was* until today. But with Mrs Wilson ill——'

'You should still have let my parents help you.'

'I earn more than enough to keep us both. The tips are excellent.'

'I bet they are!'

'And not because I let any of the customers paw me— I don't. They just chat me up.'

'I didn't imagine otherwise,' Abby said swiftly. 'It's the thought of their remarks and leering that makes my blood boil. I care about your self-respect and——'

'So do I.' Caroline dabbed at her eyes. 'But I'm not trained for office work, and I earn far more at the club than I could in a shop. That's why I can't afford to lose my job.'

'I see.' Abby chewed on her lower lip. 'OK, I'll baby-sit for you, though I'd better warn you, I've never changed a nappy.'

'I don't want you to babysit. Charlie's too fretful to be left with a stranger.'

'Then why *did* you call me?'

'To ask you to stand in for me at the club.'

Abby gasped. But a glance at her cousin's pale, set face told her she had heard correctly.

'You've got to do it for me, Abby. I get paid tonight, and if I don't turn up I might lose my money.'

Abby longed to give her some to tide her over but instinctively knew it would be the wrong thing to do.

'What makes you think they'll accept me as your stand-in?' she asked.

'They won't know.' Thin hands twisted together. 'I want them to think you're me.'

'You're kidding.'

'Why? We're the same height and our colouring's similar. The lighting's pretty dim too, and——'

'Even if I can look like you, it won't fool the other girls.'

'They're a nice bunch, and won't give me away.'

'There's still your boss. He's sure to know I'm not you.'

'He's away for a week, and the assistant manager wouldn't recognise one kitten from another. Incidentally, I'm known there as Carla. We're not called by our real names.'

'I'm not surprised,' Abby said sarcastically before she could stop herself.

'There you go again! Trying to make me feel ashamed of what I do.' Caroline began to cry, and Abby, overcome by remorse, hugged her again.

'Darling, I'm sorry. It's just that I'm upset with you for not asking us for help. But of course I'll take your place tonight.'

It wasn't until a couple of hours later, as she was dressing to do so, that Abby regretted her promise. How vulgar a kitten's clothes were! Hiding her thoughts, she pulled on a pair of sheer black tights over her long, shapely legs. A few hours ago she had never dreamed that by the end of the day she'd be dressing—or rather undressing—to be leered at by a room full of sex-hungry males! Glancing at her cousin's fine-boned features, she vowed to get her away from this dreadful club and equally dreadful apartment.

'How do I look?' Abby asked, thinking what a ridiculous figure she cut in the brief satin outfit, with its stiffy arched, fluffy cat tail protruding from the back, and equally silly fluffy ears perched on her shoulder-length hair. It was fortunate the costume fitted, for while she was almost as slender as her cousin, her shape was more voluptuous: full breasts tapering down to a tiny waist and well-rounded hips.

For answer, Caroline collapsed on the settee, choking with laughter. 'I can't believe I look as silly as you!'

'I bet you do,' Abby retorted. 'Now perhaps you'll pocket your pride and let my parents help you until you can get on your feet.'

'You're right, of course, but——'

'Not buts, Caro,' Abby insisted. 'I'll take over for you tonight, but tomorrow we'll have a serious talk regarding your future.'

CHAPTER TWO

ENTERING the smoke-filled Kitty Club, Abby was conscious of male eyes running lecherously over her scantily clad body, lingering at bare shoulders, swelling breasts, and exaggerated length of thigh below the cut-away briefs. Squirming inside, she lowered the tray of drinks to shield herself.

'Come on, honey,' a coarse voice cajoled above the near deafening blare of disco music, 'show us what you have behind the tray!'

It took a tremendous effort on Abby's part not to tip the tray and its contents over the smirking face.

'Don't let it get to you,' another 'Kitten' murmured as Abby crossed paths with her. 'Imagine what it would be like if we had to strip for them!'

'I can't,' Abby shuddered, and glancing at the men around her, wondered how Caroline could ever have taken such a job when she had an aunt and uncle willing to help her. Pride was her downfall, except it was worse than pride. Obstinacy was a better description.

'Hey, sweetie,' a boozy voice rasped at her side. 'Care to meet me after the show?'

About to tell him to go to hell, a warning glance from a Kitten nearby stopped her, as did the realisation that she had to collect Caroline's pay cheque—her last one if she had anything to do with it. There was no reason why her cousin couldn't be found work at Stewart and Stewart, her father's public relations company. She was bright enough, and was excellent training material.

'So what do you say?' the drunken voice persisted.

13

'Sorry, sir,' she purred, refusing to glance at him as she went towards a table of customers beckoning to her, 'but I'm meeting my husband.'

'How do you stand this?' she muttered to another Kitten, remembering to keep a smile on her heavily lip-sticked mouth.

'By closing my mind and thinking of my pay cheque!' came the answer.

Abby tried to do the same, but as the night wore on she was tempted to leave and pay her cousin from her own pocket. Yet if she did, Caroline was certain to find out from one of her friends at the club, and be insulted.

How had she borne the insinuating and degrading remarks of these disgusting pigs week after week, month after month? And 'disgusting' was the perfect word for them, for no self-respecting male would be seen in such a dump.

So what were those two executive types, waiting at the entrance of the gaudily decorated room, doing here? Immaculately groomed, they not only stood out like gold among dross, but in their late twenties and mid-thirties were younger than most of the other customers. Better looking too, particularly the older one. Under pretext of counting the cash on her tray, Abby watched him survey the club and its occupants with a disdainful sweep of eye, as he listened to what his companion was saying. She was even more intrigued as she saw Pete, the *maître d'*, hurry forward to show them to a table with an unrestricted view of the strip show soon to come on.

'You're not being paid to stand around,' he hissed at her a moment later as he passed in front of her. 'Go and do your stuff.' He jerked his head in the direction of the newcomers.

Abby had been too intent on observing them to remember they were sitting at one of the tables she served. The smile she had forced herself to wear all evening was instantly replaced by her natural wide one as she moved gracefully towards them with her tray.

As she went to say 'good evening' and ask them for their order, the younger, fairer man half rose and said, 'Carla!' then abruptly sat down, his expression puzzled. 'Sorry. I thought you were her. Your hair's the same colour and——'

'I *am* Carla,' she mumbled, a blush suffusing her cheeks, not only at her lie, but at the way his friend was contemptuously surveying her.

'No, you're not,' the younger man grinned as he glanced round. 'I know her too well to be fooled! Will you tell her Kevin wants to see her?'

'May I take your order?' she asked, ignoring his request and wondering how to get him alone to explain why she was standing in for Caroline.

'Scotch on the rocks,' the older man grunted, answering her question.

'I'll have a double,' Kevin added. 'And please give Carla my message.'

'Can't you see she isn't here?' This was said with ill-concealed impatience by his friend. 'So the sooner we leave the better.'

'Not until I discover where she is.'

'She left a note for you, sir,' Abby interjected speedily, addressing the fair-haired man, afraid he might ask Pete where Carla was. 'If you'd come with me...'

Not waiting for his answer, she undulated away. Her ploy worked, for he jumped up and followed her to the bar.

'She isn't well,' Abby whispered, deciding not to give him the real reason in case he didn't know of the baby. 'She asked me to stand in for her tonight because she was frightened of losing her job. You won't give her away, will you?' she added conspiratorially.

'Of course not,' he promised, frowning. 'But could I have her address to send her some flowers?'

Abby, surprised at Kevin's concern—he had to be more than a little sweet on her cousin—debated whether to give it to him. Yet wouldn't Caroline have already done so had she wanted him to know it? Unless she had been embarrassed for him to visit her in case it jeopardised her divorce? Jeffrey was just the type to hire a detective to watch her!

'She should be back in a night or two,' Abby prevaricated. 'Now if you'll return to your seat, I'll bring you your drinks.'

As he moved off, a red-headed Kitten sauntered close. 'That guy's mad keen on Carla,' she whispered. 'He's been coming here every night since he saw her here. Beats me why she won't date him. Wish *I'd* had the chance.'

'Maybe he isn't her type.'

'Are you kidding? She lights up every time he looks at her, but she won't date *anyone*.'

Abby forestalled further conversation by giving the barman her order, and while she waited for it, she half turned to take a better look at Kevin. It was obvious he was determined to see her cousin, and she was curious why a man of his apparent sophistication should have come here in the first place. Yet even as her gaze ranged over him they were drawn to his companion.

It was ages since she had met anyone who had impinged on her so strongly. His air of command set him apart from every other male here. Dark chestnut hair waved back from a high, intelligent forehead and firm nose, while a wide mouth above a pugnacious chin showed he was accustomed to having his commands obeyed. Well-defined brows drew attention to the narrowed, brooding eyes beneath, eyes that held a sensuality totally different from the leers of the other men around her. Pity he couldn't muster a smile. It would have made him even handsomer—if that were possible. Still, it was a good thing *he* wasn't the one who was keen on Caroline. With such a bad-tempered scowl on his face he wouldn't have been fobbed off as easily as Kevin.

'You the one who ordered two whiskys?' the barman said behind her, and she swung round to take them from him.

With the drinks on her tray, she went briskly across the room, evading the hands that tried to touch her and ignoring the salacious remarks continually whispered to her.

'You can't possibly know what Carla's like till you've met her,' she heard Kevin say to his companion as she came within earshot.

'I can make a damn good guess!'

'You've always said one shouldn't prejudge,' Kevin defended himself.

'It isn't a matter of prejudging,' the older man glared at him. 'But only a girl on the make would work here.'

'Rory,' Kevin warned, glancing uncomfortably at Abby.

Unperturbed, his companion favoured her with an intent stare, a faint sneer curving his lips, and Abby seethed with indignation. Regardless of what he took her for, he had no right to behave as though she had no feelings. But then he was the type who thought manners weren't required in a club like this. The glass in her hand trembled, and with an effort she resisted the urge to tip its contents over his head. That would have taught him to mind his tongue! Trouble was, it would also have got her the sack and lost Caroline the money owing to her.

Setting down the two glasses, she accepted payment from Kevin and searched in the furry purse at her waist for the change.

'Drink up and let's get the hell out of this dump,' Rory ordered the younger man, unfurling all six feet of rippling muscle.

'I might as well have a fling at roulette,' Kevin said. 'Care to join me?'

The older man's hesitation was palpable, then he shrugged. 'I guess anything's preferable to watching these bimbos.'

Again Abby resisted the urge to hit him, and stony-faced she dropped the change on to the table and walked off.

For the next half-hour she was busy serving drinks and sandwiches to a crowd of celebrating rugger fans, and was returning a stack of used glasses to the bar, when the high-pitched voice of the *maître d'* broke into her thoughts.

'Hey, you, Carla! They're short-staffed in the gaming-room. Give them a hand—on the double.'

Though resenting his tone, she nodded, not wanting to draw attention to the fact that she knew nothing of the gambling operations. It would also mean her being in the same room as Rory, but even that was preferable to the lewd glances of the customers in the club itself. Though the same ghastly types were likely to be gambling, they'd at least be intent on the spin of the roulette wheel or the cards at the chemmy table, rather than on her.

Edging past the seated, hunched figures, and the by-standers watching over their shoulders—none of whom she was relieved to see was Rory—she looked around for someone to tell her where to go and what to do. Approaching the nearest croupier, she waited till he had spun the wheel before asking him how she could assist.

'It's probably the drinks and sandwiches they want you to help with,' he told her uninterestedly, his gaze focused on the spinning wheel.

No better off for the information, Abby stepped back from him and bumped smack against a broad expanse of chest. She turned to apologise, but the words froze on her lips as she found herself staring at the one man she had hoped to avoid. Well, at least he wasn't scowling, nor did he appear irritated by the encounter.

'Following me?' he drawled, his tone maddeningly condescending.

'We're short-handed and I'm serving,' she said flatly, tilting her head and staring straight into his eyes. 'May I bring you a drink?'

Unexpectedly his expression softened, and her heart went into over-drive at sight of the curving mouth and the dark grey eyes that were suddenly friendly instead of hostile.

'A coffee, please. Black and strong if you don't mind.'

Mind? She'd make it herself if necessary! Dazed, she headed across to the swinging door indicating the kitchen.

Within minutes she was back, tapping him lightly on the shoulder as he bent to say something to Kevin at the table.

'Three pounds, please, sir.' She had forgotten to ask how much to charge, and knowing it was the price in the club itself, decided it would be the same in the casino.

'*Three pounds*?' he echoed.

His tone was aggressive and she wondered why. She also wondered at the hardening of his mouth, when it had been smiling at her a moment ago. Could she have charged too much? Even if she had, the difference was pennies, and unless he was particularly tight-fisted, why was he so angry?

'Yes, sir,' Abby answered.

'Got yourself a nice little racket here, haven't you?' The quietness of his tone was menacing.

'I—I don't understand.'

'I'd have thought it was simple enough. You're trying to make yourself some money on the side.'

'I——'

'Don't you know a casino doesn't charge for coffee?' he elaborated.

Abby gave an exclamation. What an idiot she was to forget! Of course they didn't. Food and drink, including alcohol, were free in the casino.

'I'm sorry,' she apologised, 'but this is the first time I've worked in here.'

'If you're going to lie, at least think of something more original,' he grated, and taking a five-pound note from his pocket, tossed it on to her tray. 'Keep the change. You obviously need it.'

Resisting the urge to throw the coins back at him, Abby decided to drop the money into a charity box.

Kevin motioned to him and murmured something. It must have been a request for money, for the older man took a wad of notes from his wallet and handed them over before wending his way towards the exit. Clearly he was bored and had decided to leave.

'Get me a whisky and soda, will you, luv?' a man nearby called to her.

Turning to comply, she felt a soft, bulky object underfoot. Glancing down, she saw it was the black crocodile wallet Rory had taken from his pocket to give Kevin the money. It must have slipped out as he put it back!

Her first instinct was to leave it where it was. It would serve him right if someone less principled than herself found it and kept it. On the other hand, what better way of embarrassing him than by proving her honesty? Fortunately he had stopped to chat to a man by the casino door, so she would have the pleasure of seeing his discomfiture when she handed it to him. Retrieving the wallet from the floor, she hurried across to him.

'I think this is yours?' she said, her voice dripping honey, as she handed him the wallet.

Expecting contrition, she was badly mistaken.

'It is,' he confirmed ungraciously. 'But how did *you* get hold of it?'

'If you're implying I picked your pocket...'

He did not deny the accusation, and anger swamped her. But she managed to keep control.

'It was lying on the floor near the roulette table,' she said acidly.

'Really?' The tone was disbelieving, and to add insult to injury he riffled through the contents. 'Nothing appears to be missing,' he conceded, his eyes staring directly into hers. The subdued lighting had made the pupils dilate and the irises were just a fine silver rim around them. 'Clearly you deserve a reward.' He extracted a twenty-pound note and held it out to her.

'Honesty is its own reward,' she replied cuttingly, and with a toss of her head, stalked off.

She was halfway across the room when a stout, swarthy man blocked her path.

'Who the hell are you?' he demanded.

'Carla,' she answered abruptly, in an attempt to discourage any small talk.

'Who are you trying to kid?' A pudgy hand gripped the soft flesh of her upper arm, and forcing her to keep pace with him, he marched her to a quiet spot on the far side of the room. 'I know every girl I hire,' he grunted, 'and unless you've had overnight plastic surgery, Carla you're not!'

Guessing he was Vincent, the assistant manager, Abby had no option but to admit the truth. 'I'm her c-cousin,' she stammered. 'Carla's ill and asked me to stand in for her. She didn't want to let you down.'

'You mean she didn't want to lose her pay,' he corrected with a sneer. 'But she's done OK swopping with you. As replacements go you're not half bad.' Beady eyes ranged from breasts to hips to thighs. 'If you're nice to me, I might be willing to keep you on permanently.'

Nauseated by the suggestion, she attempted to wrench herself free. But to no avail, for he tightened his hold.

'I admire a bit of spunk,' he leered. 'The ones who say "yes" too quickly are no fun.'

'I'd never say "yes" to you,' she snapped. 'If you don't let go of me, I'll scream,' she warned.

'I'm sure it won't be necessary,' Rory's voice said behind her, his strong fingers prising Vincent's from her arm. 'No gentleman detains a lady against her will.' Typically of the man, there was sarcastic emphasis on the words 'gentleman' and 'lady'.

'In this establishment, the customer is always right,' Vincent said with forced *bonhomie* as he backed away.

'Nice people you work for,' Rory murmured. 'It was lucky I noticed what was going on.'

'Thank you,' she managed tightly, still smarting from his insulting inflexion on the world 'lady'.

He shrugged wide, powerful shoulders. 'I hope you've learned a lesson. Next time you're accosted there might not be anyone around to rescue you.' Finely curved dark eyebrows drew together. 'Not that you deserve it. You doll yourself up to turn men on and act the squeamish virgin when you succeed.'

'I clearly don't turn *you* on,' she answered pointedly. 'But no doubt you're a saint!'

'Let's just say I'm not attracted to a girl that one has to pay for one's pleasures.'

'How *dare* you?' Forgetting Caroline in her fury, Abby's hand came out and slapped his face with all her strength.

A red blotch appeared on his cheek, and slowly he touched his fingers to it.

'I thought face-slapping went out with bustles,' he said with surprising calm. 'But maybe you mistook your furry tail for one!'

'The only thing I mistook was *you*—for Sir Galahad!' she retorted. 'Next time you rescue a damsel in distress, perhaps you'll manage to be more gracious.'

Near to tears, she fled into the cloakroom and collapsed on a stool.

What a nightmare helping her cousin had proved to be. She had been ogled, pawed, propositioned and insulted, and the evening was not yet finished! She had no idea how she was going to get through the remaining hours, but for Caroline's sake she had to stick it out. There was still her pay cheque to collect.

Sighing, she rose and made her way back into the casino.

CHAPTER THREE

ENTERING her father's office at nine next morning, Abby collapsed into the leather chair in front of his desk.

'You'd make a good advert for the morning after the night before!' he commented, setting aside the newspaper he had been reading.

'Thanks,' she muttered. 'There's nothing like flattery to make a girl feel great.'

'Don't tell me you were burning the midnight oil on the Smallwood contract?'

She shook her head.

'Then why the dark circles?'

With an eager rush of words, Abby gave him a quick resumé of the events of the previous evening, omitting all mention of Rory. To do so would raise her father's blood-pressure higher than it already was, if sight of his annoyed expression was anything to go by.

'What a damned stupid thing to do!' he exclaimed. 'Going to a place like that!'

'I did it to help Caroline.'

'Supposing one of our clients had seen you there?'

'It isn't a place our clients go to. It's a real dump. And if one of them *had* been there, they'd never have recognised me!' she grinned. Now that the experience was over, she thought of it with equanimity, amusement even. 'Anyway, it isn't our clients we should be concerned with, it's Caroline.'

'You're right. She must leave that job at once and move in with your mother and me—at least till she can afford a decent place of her own,' Mr Stewart said immediately. 'We can find her something to do here. We'll be needing extra help with the Smallwood contract.'

'Exactly my thought!' Abby jumped up. 'I just wanted to hear you say it.'

'As if you needed to!' he replied, his eyes softening fondly as they rested on his only child. 'But thanks anyway. It's good to know I still have some say in the running of my company!'

She blew him a kiss. 'I'll call Caroline right away and then fix an appointment to see Mr Smallwood.'

'You'll have to handle him carefully,' her father reminded her.

'Quit worrying. I promise I'll flatter his ego and smooth his feathers!' Abby refused to let herself be intimidated by chairmen, no matter how intimidating they appeared.

'Let me know how you get on with him.'

In her office, where the stark black and white décor and vivid touches of turquoise and lime-green were a direct contrast to the conventionally bland colouring of her father's, she immediately called her cousin.

'I have your money,' she said, cutting through her thanks. 'And it's the last you'll earn from the club. From now on you're working here.'

'But——'

'No buts. We've just taken on an enormous contract and we'll have to engage extra staff. What's more, you can go on flexi-time, as well as doing work for us at home.'

'You and Uncle Arthur are too generous,' Caroline gulped. 'I don't know a thing about public relations, and you're just trying to fit me in.'

'Sure we are,' Abby agreed, realising it was futile to lie. 'But we really will have to take on several people, and you happen to be bright enough to learn quickly.'

'What will I have to do?'

'Mail promotion shots to begin with. But if you've an aptitude for publicity you may be able to write some of the stuff yourself.' Abby broke off. 'I haven't the time to elaborate now—it's too involved. Let's just leave it that you're coming to work for us.'

The line was silent for a moment. 'OK,' Caroline said, 'if you really feel you need me, I'd love to accept.'

'Great.' Abby sensed the younger girl's relief, and was delighted she had sorted out one aspect of her life. 'By the way,' she added, 'some guy named Kevin was looking for you last night.'

'Oh? Wh-what did you tell him about me?'

'That you weren't well and I was taking your place. I didn't mention the baby because I wasn't sure if he knew you had one.'

'He doesn't. Tell me, what did you think of Kevin?'

'Compared with the other men in the club he seemed quite nice,' Abby replied, thinking this didn't mean much. 'Have you ever dated him?' she checked, uncertain whether the other Kitten's information last night was true.

'No. I made it a point never to date customers. Anyway, I'm in no position to see anyone, what with the baby and Jeffrey.'

'Jeffrey? What business is it of his who you see?'

'None, but he can still make trouble.'

Abby was surprised. She had assumed her cousin had finished with her husband, but did not press the issue.

'I'm sorry for Kevin,' the girl said unexpectedly. 'He seems a lonely person. His father's dead and he has a sister a year or so older than himself.'

'He wasn't alone yesterday. He came in with an older man called Rory.'

'He's a great friend,' her cousin said with some animation. 'I've never met him but Kevin often speaks of him. He's a sort of older brother figure. I wish I'd been there to see him.'

Abby doubted whether the girl's feelings would have been reciprocated by Kevin's grim-faced companion, but again held her tongue. Indeed she'd held it so often the past twelve hours that it was feeling sore!

'Was Rory nice?' Caroline went on.

'He has rather fixed ideas and is used to getting his own way. Look, I must dash. I've a stack of things to do. We'll expect you here Monday morning at nine-thirty, providing you can find someone to take care of Charlie,' she added, suddenly remembering the baby. Although her father had said he wanted Caroline to move back with them, she decided it was best if he or her mother proffered the invitation.

'There's a local crèche I can try,' the younger girl said. 'But if they don't have any room I'll be stuck.'

'Can't your landlady help? The company always pays for babycare.'

'I doubt that! I won't——'

'For heaven's sake swallow your pride. We're giving you the opportunity to make a career for yourself, so take it.'

'I—I don't know what to say.'

'The word is "yes". And we'll see you Monday.'

Replacing the receiver, Abby picked it up immediately to continue with her next call. Half an hour later she had completed them and, pen in hand, began planning her strategy for the Smallwood account.

It was six p.m. before she had finished and sent the report by special messenger to Mr Smallwood's home, having first checked with his secretary that this was acceptable to him.

'Yes indeed,' the woman had said. 'Then he'll be well briefed for his meeting with you.'

Now, aware of a job well done, Abby leaned back in her chair with a sigh of relief. Tired from the long day and her sleepless night, she was delighted it was Friday; she had the whole weekend in which to relax until Monday, when she would be discussing her ideas with their new client.

The weekend flew by, filled with a party on Saturday and an early movie and dinner on Sunday with Martin Buchanan, her current boyfriend. A successful director of television commercials, he was divorced and had no children. She had met him three months ago, and though he was attractive and fun to be with, she knew he could never mean anything special to her. The trouble was no other man had either, and guilt-ridden by her parents' obvious desire for her to marry and give them grandchildren, she sometimes wondered if she was being too choosy. After all, she was twenty-six, and far too level-headed to expect to be swept off her feet by a knight in shining armour.

Yet that was exactly what she was still hoping for. In an age when love was sneered at as a requirement for sex, she was old-fashioned enough to believe it was necessary. Her girlfriends fell in and out of bed in the same casual manner their mothers had bestowed chaste kisses a generation ago, and Abby was teased for her prim and proper stance. But she was far from either. She had tried their way and found it wanting. True, it had only been on one occasion, but her inability to respond had confirmed her beliefs, and even now, three years later, she had not forgotten the recriminations of her partner, who had drawn away from her in anger and accused her of being frigid.

Arriving at work on Monday morning, she found Caroline already seated behind her newly assigned desk, sorting through a stack of information on Smallwood's.

'I managed to get Charlie into the crèche,' she smiled, 'and my landlady will collect him at three and take care of him till I get back. So if you ever want me to stay on late, I can.'

'Great. See how easy it is to organise things if you're given a little push? Nothing is impossible if one tries hard enough.'

'I don't agree. It's often a question of timing or luck.'

'It's too early in the day to be philosophical,' Abby grinned, twirling round in front of her cousin. 'How do I look for my meeting with Mr Smallwood?'

'In that outfit you'd melt the heart of a misogynist!'

Abby was glad to hear it. She had spent considerable time studying her wardrobe before deciding on a compromise between her father's staid advice and her more trendy inclination. A navy and white chalk-striped trouser suit ensured her knees were covered, while the narrow cut emphasised the slender curves of hips and legs. Beneath, a white cashmere polo-necked sweater was the perfect foil for the full curve of her breasts, and a navy Chanel bag and shoes completed the picture of executive efficiency.

'There's one thing wrong,' her cousin proffered tentatively. 'Your hair.'

Abby nodded glumly. 'I know, I know. I shouldn't let it hang long and loose.'

'Not unless you want Mr Smallwood to start pawing the ground and neighing!'

'The neighing I can cope with—it's the no-ing I don't want!'

Going into the cloakroom, she pulled her long, thick red-gold coloured hair away from her face, plaiting it loosely and then rolling it into a coil to rest on the nape of her neck. Yes, she had to admit her cousin was correct. It *did* complete the picture of efficiency she was aiming to create.

She was even more pleased with herself when she met Henry Smallwood's prim secretary, for the woman flashed her a look of approval as she showed her into her employer's oak-panelled office.

'Delighted to meet you, Miss Stewart,' a grey-haired man in his late sixties greeted her, a friendly smile on his lined face as he fussily arranged a chair for her beside a low coffee-table, made certain she was comfortable, and enquired if she preferred coffee to tea, before sitting opposite her.

Listening to him, Abby marvelled that he was chairman of a country-wide chain. With his old-world courtliness and pernickety manner, it was easy to see why—if attitudes were reflected from the boardroom downwards—the group needed new blood and a more modern image. True, it had a reputation for giving value for money, but profits were poor in relation to turnover, exacerbated by too large a staff, many of whom were well past their sell-by date!

Confidently she waited as he opened the file in front of him and riffled through the pages of her report. From experience she knew she would have no problem handling this old dear who, she was certain, owed his position more to inheritance than ability. Men of his type were more open to advice than self-made businessmen who jealously guarded their brain-children from outside influences.

'There are some good ideas in here, Miss Stewart, particularly where you propose giving our staff a specific image and bringing them closer to the general public. "We care—you buy",' he quoted her slogan with a smile. 'Catchy, short, and easy to remember. However, my opinion is no longer the one that counts.'

Abby's spirits plunged. 'It isn't?'

'No. The man you will have to persuade is Rossiter Hunt. Don't look dismayed, my dear. I'm sure he'll admire your proposals as much as I do. He's extremely go-ahead and we're lucky to have him with us—even though we had to buy his company to achieve it.'

'When did this happen?' Abby asked, alarm bells ringing. It appeared as if things were not going to be as straightforward as she had hoped.

'The final papers were signed on Thursday and the press release goes out this afternoon. You're in the fortunate position of being the first to hear of it.' Henry Smallwood fiddled with his coffee-cup. 'We are a family controlled firm, and some of our younger members felt their capital might be more gainfully employed elsewhere. If they had sold their shares, we would have run the risk of being taken over by a predator, so the family decided to become a predator itself!' He smiled happily. 'We needed stronger management, and by buying the Coopers' chain we've got it.'

Abby nodded. Coopers' was often described as a young Marks and Spencer, and had a similar reputation for excellent quality and service. Smallwood's must have paid well over the odds to buy them.

'Shall I contact Mr Hunt myself, or would you prefer to introduce me?' she asked.

'It would be better if I did it.' Mr Smallwood seemed slightly discomfited. 'You see, when I had discussions with your father I wasn't aware Rossiter would be against us using an outside firm for our public relations. He believes it can be done equally well within our own organisation—as he's been doing with Coopers'.'

With an effort Abby kept her cool. 'It's easier to promote the image of a successful chain.'

'Yes, yes,' came the hurried retort. 'But Coopers' wasn't *always* successful. They were doing badly until Rossiter joined them. He was a lawyer, and nephew of the founder, and when his uncle appealed to him for help, he took over. Coopers' recovery was one of the success stories of the eighties, and when old Cedric died he bequeathed it to his nephew.'

One of Abby's delicate eyebrows rose. 'So the law was shelved and big business took over permanently?'

Henry Smallwood folded liver-mottled hands on his stomach. 'At first, Rossiter wanted to sell out and return to law, but because of his late uncle he felt guilty at doing it.'

'That speaks well for him,' Abby conceded, surprised by such sentiment from an obviously hard-headed businessman. Her interest in meeting him increased.

'He'll breathe new life into our stores too,' Mr Smallwood continued, 'though the first task is to integrate the two groups. We've concentrated on clothing and household goods, so it will mean adding food sections.' The grey head nodded. 'There is really a great deal to be done.'

'And a totally new image to project,' Abby stated. 'Which is where *we* can help.'

Indeed, the more she learned of the task ahead of the newly amalgamated group, the happier she was, for it could be her biggest and most important client, and a marvellous opportunity for her to show her ability.

'I haven't told Rossiter a woman will be handling our PR,' Mr Smallwood cut into her thoughts. 'Merely that we've engaged your firm. He assumes he'll be working with your father.'

'My father only handles City institutions,' Abby said, disappointed that Mr Hunt—who sounded so impressive—appeared to be a chauvinist.

'He's intelligent enough to appreciate your ability as soon as he reads this report of yours,' came the reassuring reply.

'But not so intelligent that he isn't prejudiced,' Abby remarked, and wondered what the ambitious younger man made of Henry Smallwood's staider approach to

business. The clash of behavioural styles in any organisation often proved a major obstacle to its smooth
running, and she had no wish to be caught in the middle.

'I'll be stepping out of the picture once I've in-
troduced you to Rossiter,' the older man went on, putting
her mind at ease. 'But since my company had originally
engaged yours, it seemed right for me to meet you and
explain the new set-up.'

Pressing the intercom on his desk, he asked his secretary to put him through to Mr Hunt. Within a few
seconds a deep, slightly impatient voice, reverberated in
the room.

'You wanted me, Henry?'

'Yes. You remember I mentioned I had engaged a PR
firm? Well Miss Stewart is with me now, and I wondered
if you had time to see her? I've read her report and pro-
jection and find it most interesting.'

'Ask her to contact my secretary and set up a meeting,'
came the reluctant reply. 'I can spare her a quarter of
an hour, so warn her not to be long-winded.'

'Do you mind if I have a word with Mr Hunt myself?'
Abby whispered softly and, when Mr Smallwood
nodded, she leaned across the desk and spoke into the
intercom.

'This is Abby Stewart, Mr Hunt. I appreciate you're
extremely busy, but frankly, if you can't spare me more
than quarter of an hour, there isn't any point in our
meeting. Unless I learn to speed-speak there's no way I
can present my ideas in fifteen minutes!'

'Point taken, Miss Stewart,' he said curtly.

'Does that mean I get half an hour at least?' she shot
back at once.

'Providing you don't mind an early start to your
morning. Seven-thirty Thursday suit you?'

'I can make it earlier if you wish. I usually begin work
at seven,' she lied sweetly.

'No—seven-thirty's fine. Breakfast at my apartment, Two, Radley House, Mayfair.'

Pre-empting her agreement, the intercom went dead.

'He's not usually so abrupt,' Henry Smallwood excused with obvious embarrassment. 'He has a lot on his mind at the moment.'

'I hope he'll have more after I've seen him!' Abby replied.

'Well, you certainly appear to have found the right formula for handling him! Good luck on Thursday, my dear.'

As Abby drove back to her office, she knew more than luck was required to convince Rossiter Hunt that Stewart and Stewart were capable of doing the work he wanted. If she failed, he was tough enough to find some legal loophole to get him out of the contract Henry Smallwood had signed.

Storming into her office, she called for Caroline to come in on the double.

'I can see your meeting went well,' her cousin said. 'You're firing on all cylinders. Was the chairman that impressive?'

'Huh! He's an ineffective old dear who should have retired years ago.' Concisely she recounted everything that had happened.

'You've nothing to worry about,' Caroline said staunchly. 'When Mr Hunt reads your report he'll be eating out of your hand.'

'Or biting it off!' Abby frowned. 'None of the ideas I put forward apply to the Coopers' group—they're a different ball game—and if I want to impress Mr Hunt, which I do, I'll have to show him that making a success of his own group doesn't mean he knows it all. In three days' time I'm going to make him realise he has a hell of a lot to learn, and that I'm the one who can teach him!'

'Teach him?'

'How to improve his stores.'

'You can't be serious! Their lay-out makes them a delight to shop in, and their merchandise is wonderful and competitively priced.'

'Is that so?' Abby picked up her purse. 'Then let's go.'

'Where?' Caroline asked breathlessly as she raced along the corridor, trying to keep up with her cousin's long, graceful strides.

'To see as many outlets as possible, and show you how wrong you are! I'm going to find faults with them if it kills me! Mr Hunt needs cutting down to size and I'll enjoy wielding the axe!'

By mid-afternoon the two girls had traipsed from end to end of the three most prestigious Coopers' in Oxford Street, Knightsbridge, and Kensington, and Abby was fast coming to the conclusion that the great Rossiter Hunt might conceivably be right, and didn't have a thing to learn!

'Let's call it a day,' Caroline groaned, easing off a shoe and rubbing her instep. 'My feet are telling me to sit down, and my instincts are telling me you aren't going to find anything wrong with this group.'

'I'm not giving in yet,' Abby said firmly. 'It's late-night shopping in some of the suburbs, and that's where we're going.'

But here too no faults were to be found. The staff were courteous and enthusiastic without being pushy, the merchandise was identical in every outlet, and the choice of clothes and food as varied in Neasden as in Knightsbridge. No wonder so many women regarded Coopers' as indispensable.

'I haven't noticed one thing that should be changed or improved,' complained Caroline wearily, as they returned to the darkened office at nine that evening.

'I agree with you,' Abby admitted. 'And since we can't fault what they do, let's see if we can fault what they don't!' Dropping her bag on her desk, she sat down and drew a sheet of paper towards her.

'You aren't thinking of working *now*, are you?' her cousin demanded.

'I sure am. I work best when my mind's fresh.'

'It can't be fresh at this hour!'

'Yes, it is. It's pumping with adrenalin—and whenever I think of Rossiter Hunt, it starts pumping more!'

'Then you won't be needing a cup of black coffee?'

'Too right. I'd like a pot! Will you be an angel and make one?'

Mumbling, 'Slave labour,' though grinning as she did, Caroline went off to do as she was bid.

CHAPTER FOUR

THE sun was sparkling on the soft green lawn and early flowering shrubs outside Abby's bedroom window as she pulled open the curtains at six o'clock on Thursday morning. Though it was early March, spring was in the air, and this was reflected in the warmer than average temperature for the time of year.

Tossing aside the cobweb of red-gold curls tumbling round her face, she padded into the bathroom and turned the shower to cool. Stepping out of her silk nightdress, she drew a deep breath and plunged bravely into the water with a screech of shock.

Minutes later, wide awake and tingling, she slid open her wardrobe and surveyed the clothes hanging there. This interview was going to be more difficult than the one with Henry Smallwood, and she wished she knew more about Mr Hunt than his business acumen.

'Off to the races, are we?' the young gardener asked admiringly, squinting up from the herbaceous border he was weeding outside her six-flat conversion in a large Victorian mansion in Highgate.

'Not quite,' she grinned, momentarily assailed by doubts as to the wisdom of her outfit as she climbed into her car. Wary of marking the winter-white skirt and complementing grey check jacket, she settled gingerly on the seat and fastened the safety-belt. As she did, she glimpsed the cleavage between her breasts. Bother! She'd meant to tighten the inside button, and must remember not to lean forward during breakfast—particularly as the man with whom she'd be sharing it would enjoy making a meal of her!

One good thing about an early meeting, she mused as she turned into the Edgware Road, was that there was no trouble finding a meter. Parking directly outside Mr Hunt's marble- and glass-fronted apartment block, she pressed the video entryphone.

Though outwardly the picture of confidence in the St Laurent outfit that had set her back a month's salary in their sale—Abby refused to accept financial help from her father and lived on her earnings—her courage slowly ebbed when there was no answer to her ring. Had Mr Hunt forgotten their appointment, or worse still deliberately chosen to? She went to ring again, but before her hand reached the button, the videophone flashed into operation and a disembodied voice asked her to come to the top floor.

Stepping out of the lift a moment later, she found herself opposite a glossy black double door that was promptly opened by a white-coated Filipino manservant.

'Please to follow me,' he invited in almost accentless English.

Abby followed him down a thickly carpeted corridor into a green and white dining-room, whose trellis-patterned walls and hand-painted lacquered furniture gave the impression of being outdoors. The blending of background and furnishings and the subtle harmonies of the colours were suggestive of a professional hand, yet there were so many personal touches it somehow contradicted this effect. Behind the sliding glass doors at the end was a large, tiled terrace filled with a brilliant profusion of flowers, while beyond was a clear view of the skyline of south-west London, and the variegated greenery of Hyde Park.

A heavy, oval glass table, large enough to seat twelve, was set with floral china—whose pattern she recognised as Minton—a bubbling percolator and a large bowl of fresh fruit.

'Please make yourself comfortable. Mr Hunt won't be long,' the man said, and glided through an adjoining door.

The kitchen, she guessed, as the movement wafted a tantalising aroma of fresh-baked croissants into the room. It would be great if her new client surprised her and turned out to be as pleasant as his staff and surroundings. Maybe when they had spoken on the telephone he had been in an unusually bad humour.

Footsteps behind made her turn, and the disbelief on the face of the man standing on the threshold told her that his mood, if anything, was going to be even worse.

'*You*?' a deep baritone boomed.

Momentarily speechless, Abby finally managed a hoarse, 'Oh, no!' as she recognised the arrogant man from the Kitty Club, who had accused her of being a thief!

'What the hell are you doing here?' The white shirt-sleeved figure took a step towards her, and nervous of his aggressive tone she shrank back. 'If this is Kevin's idea of a joke, you can tell him I don't appreciate his humour.'

'Nor would I if this *were* a joke,' Abby replied, her fear receding as logic told her that, thinking as he did, he had every reason to be annoyed. 'I'm Abby Stewart, and we have a breakfast meeting.'

Annoyance changed to incredulity, and he drew himself up to his full height. A veritable Goliath of a man, she thought, her new-found confidence ebbing as eyes the pale grey of frozen pools in winter moved slowly over her, the grey darkening as they filled with curiosity.

'Are you any relation to your chairman?' he enquired.

'His daughter.'

'How come you were moonlighting at that goddamn awful club? Doesn't Daddy pay you enough?'

Colour flamed in her cheeks. 'I'm a director of the firm and I earn more than enough,' she snapped. 'But he doesn't go around telling me what I can or cannot do. I'm old enough to decide for myself.'

'In which case we've nothing further to discuss,' Rossiter Hunt stated. 'You can hardly expect me to take seriously a girl who works at the Kitty Club in her spare time.'

Abby fought to control her temper. 'Even Judge Jeffreys gave prisoners a hearing before passing sentence; don't you think you should do the same?'

He eyed her stonily. So he must look at an adversary in business, she thought, and half turned from him, her profile etched against the wall: small, tip-tilted nose, mouth sweetly curved and full, but the softly rounded chin firm with indignation.

'You're quite right, Miss Stewart,' came the startling admission. 'Please sit down and give me an explanation.'

He pointed a well-manicured hand to a chair at the dining table, and after she was seated settled himself opposite her. 'Out with it,' he said, accompanying the words with a smile that transformed his face.

Abby's foolish heart did the quickstep. When austere and aloof, he had been exceptionally handsome, but when he smiled he was devastating! Yet his volte-face seemed out of character—or at least the little she knew of it—and she decided to treat this new mood with caution.

'The only reason I went to the club was to stand in for my cousin Caroline, who was—who was ill,' she explained. 'She's the "Carla" your friend Kevin came to see.'

'The girl who's so different from the rest!' he murmured with ill-concealed sarcasm.

'She is.'

'Really? Is that why she's happy to dress up as a Kitten and let herself be ogled by any Tom, Dick or Harry?'

'She's doing—she did it for the money.'

'Now *that* I believe.'

'Acting judge and jury again, are we?' Abby said sweetly.

'Sorry.' He didn't sound it. 'I'm sure she's a fine upstanding member of the community, and is only working there to help keep her aged parents in the necessities of life!'

This was more than Abby could tolerate. 'Her parents died when she was a child, and she happens to be working to keep her *baby* in necessities. Her husband deserted her and she was too proud to ask my father—her uncle—for help. Her son was ill and she rang me in desperation to take her place at the club. Until then, neither my parents nor myself knew where she lived or what she was doing. She took the job because it enabled her to be with Charlie during the day, and her landlady could take care of him at night.'

The silence was heavy and oppressive, and Abby would willingly have choked to death before breaking it.

'Seems I owe you and your cousin another apology,' Rossiter Hunt stated, clasping his hands together on the glass table, the long fingers intertwining one with the other. 'I assume *you* won't be playing the role of Kitten again?'

'You assume correctly. And neither will my cousin.'

'Don't blame me for checking. I don't want our group associated with a PR firm with questionable connections.'

'I understand,' Abby spoke through gritted teeth, still smarting that he should have thought her to be a girl who could moonlight at such a club. 'Our clients are triple A, Mr Hunt, and so is our reputation.'

He gave her a direct look—he seemed to favour them—and she met it squarely.

'I believe you, Miss Stewart. But for my peace of mind, if your cousin gets into a jam again, don't help her out!'

'Caroline's working for us now,' Abby informed him, and saw his well-defined dark eyebrows draw together in a frown.

'Then do me a favour and keep her out of Kevin's way. He has a habit of falling for the wrong woman, and I'm tired of getting him out of trouble.'

Abby's anger, not yet cooled, started bubbling. 'The boot's on the other foot, Mr Hunt. Kevin's the one who's been doing the chasing, and Caroline the running away.'

'I'm pleased to hear it. Now let's forget——'

'Nor is she a "wrong" woman,' Abby cut across him. 'She had a darn good reason for working at the club—and a damn sight better one than Kevin had for going there in the first place. So don't throw stones if you live in a glass house!'

'It isn't *my* glass house, Miss Stewart, but I take the point.' The grin was in evidence again. 'I won't apologise a third time, though, so take it as said.' He pressed a bell beneath the table with his foot. 'What's your first name?'

'Abby,' she snapped. 'And I thought yours was Rory. That's what Kevin called you.'

'He was a three-year-old when we met, and Rossiter was too much for him. So Rory it's been ever since. But no one else calls me that.'

Abby could think of other names more suitable, but swallowed them all as the manservant wheeled in a laden trolley.

Pitchers of orange and pineapple juice were placed on the table, together with a silver dish and jug containing milk and muesli, as well as a plate of hot croissants and a selection of home-made jams.

'We'll serve ourselves, thanks, Giorgio,' her host said, favouring her with another keen look. 'Don't stand on ceremony, Miss Stewart. Take what you like.'

What she would like was a sedative and an aspirin, but she had no intention of giving him that satisfaction, and poured out a glass of pineapple juice.

As she sipped it, sunshine flooded through the sliding glass doors, bathing the room in a golden glow. But Abby's mood remained grey, and she wished she were in a position to tell Rossiter Hunt what he could do with his account! Just being in his company set her hackles rising, and heaven knew how she'd be able to cope with working with him on a daily, or even weekly basis.

'Relax,' he ordered. 'You look like a lamb going to the slaughter.'

And you the wolf hoping to gobble me up! she thought, lowering long-lashed eyes in case he guessed what she was thinking. He was perceptive enough. Forcing herself to take a croissant, she nibbled it as he consumed a bowl of muesli, a peach, and three croissants spread with apricot jam.

'I'll lay odds you aren't a breakfast girl,' he remarked, replenishing their coffee-cups.

'Not on this scale,' she agreed.

'Then don't feel obliged to eat. Just because I occasionally sound like Judge Jeffreys, it doesn't mean I behave like him!'

'Thanks for the reassurance. At one stage, I definitely felt the rope round my neck!'

He chuckled, his hands, large but finely shaped, moving in a gesture of apology.

'Now that's settled, perhaps you'd care to tell me how you intend improving our image. I read your proposals for Smallwood's, but they don't apply to Coopers'.' Pushing aside his cup, he was all business as he leaned forward, his expression intent.

Abby found her eyes disconcertingly straying to his broad shoulders and the solid outline of muscles beneath the fine cotton of his shirt.

'I intend to do what any good public relations firm would do,' she said.

'I'm afraid I don't know what that is. Until now, I've luckily managed to steer clear of them.'

An angry spurt of adrenalin shot through her, but she knew it was imperative to keep her cool.

'I suppose you work on female intuition?' he continued blandly.

'Even if I do, my intuition would warn me not to admit it to *you*.'

His wide mouth quirked. 'Quick-witted as well as beautiful. What other assets do you possess?'

'The ability to stick to the point—namely that you invited me to a business meeting, not to discuss personal attributes.' Staring directly into his eyes, she was almost caught off balance by the laser-sharp glint in the silver grey depths. 'I work extremely hard, and——'

'I don't doubt it. But recalling your appearance the other evening, you look better suited to playing.'

Her green eyes clawed at him. 'I do *everything* well, Mr Hunt, but I'm particularly fussy with whom I play.'

'So am I, so we have one thing in common.'

His tone implied it was the only thing they had in common, and she began to kiss the contract goodbye.

'From the report I read,' he continued, 'you know your job and are logical and clear-thinking, but I don't need you to tell me how to run my business.'

'I've no intention of doing so—except for our particular aspect of it,' Abby replied.

'I suppose you believe you could improve the image of the Queen?' he commented drily.

'Nothing's sacrosanct.'

'My decisions are.'

'Are you too rigid to ever change your mind?'

'Not at all. But I dislike being coerced or manipulated.'

Wondering what his reaction would be if she poured one of the pitchers of fruit juice over his head, she said gently, 'If my putting forward new ideas for your group is considered coercion, then I plead guilty.'

'If you had come here wearing a sack, and a brown paper bag over your head, I wouldn't consider it coercion.'

'*What*?'

'Your sex appeal, Miss Stewart. It isn't conducive to logical thinking in a red-blooded male.' He paused, head on one side. 'Though come to think of it, perhaps the thoughts are *very* logical.'

This was altogether too much to stomach, and she pushed back her chair and rose. 'Clearly, Mr Hunt, you are wasting my time. I'm sorry I made the mistake of taking you seriously.'

She was halfway across the room when he reached her side and caught her arm.

'I was out of order, Miss Stewart. Accept my apologies.' He drew her back to her chair. 'Truth is, I'm irritated with Henry for engaging your company when he was already negotiating to buy my services. He knew damn well I have always done my own promotional work. Successfully, too.'

'Could you tell me what your plans are?' Abby asked without inflexion.

'To take Smallwood's up-market so they fit in with my group.'

'What a pity.' Abby threw caution aside, knowing it was now or never to make her point. 'The élitist market is a diminishing one.'

'Harrods wouldn't agree with you.'

'They don't run a chain like yours. If you want to retain an up-market image, set a few outlets aside for the purpose. But the bulk of them should cater for young and old, rich and poor.'

She saw his wide shoulders tense with annoyance, and registering the strength of them, knew how easily his powerful arms could crush her.

'You've done a fantastic job so far,' she hurried on, 'but time doesn't stand still and neither should a company. Don't play pop music in all the clothes areas, the way you do now, but only in those that cater for the teens and early twenties, and bring in something middle-of-the-road for the rest. I also think you should expand the young children's side. When mothers shop for themselves, they'll be only too pleased if they can also shop for the family.'

'I've been thinking of *that*,' came the admission. 'As well as crèches to make parents' own shopping less of a hassle.'

'A great idea!' she encouraged.

'Henry Smallwood will have a fit.'

'Not when he sees the profits. And remember, he bought your group to get your brains, so he'll be expecting big changes.'

Strong white teeth flashed in a smile. 'You have a persuasive line of argument, Miss Stewart, and most of what you've said I've already been considering.'

'Is that so?'

'You can see the blueprints if you like.' His grey eyes gleamed. 'So why do I need you? It would be cheaper for me to break the contract and pay you compensation.'

This was what she had feared and, knowing she had nothing to lose, she was totally honest.

'Cheaper certainly, but also stupid. Doing your own public relations means you have to devote time to thinking up schemes and then watching over them to ensure they're done properly, and I happen to think your time could be better spent. Our company will liaise with you fully, but *we* will dream up the ideas and all you will have to do is approve or veto them. Now you have amalgamated with Smallwood's, you have a lot more to get across to the public. Remember, Coopers' will lose some of its trendy customers and Smallwood's some of its stuffy ones, but with the proper publicity you can quickly regain that loss.'

'That's why I pay my advertising agency.'

'The publicity we bring our clients isn't bought advertising,' she plunged on. 'We get articles written about you and your company—put some of your personnel on TV, organise competitions and promotions. Publicity is a snowball, Mr Hunt—once it starts rolling it gains momentum. No matter how good your advertising agency, they think in a different way from us.'

'What personnel would you promote?' he asked.

'*You* for a start,' she said boldly. 'You've made Coopers' a household name and I'd like to see *you* as a household personality.'

'Never. I value my privacy too much. The last thing I want is to walk down the street giving autographs!'

She smiled, her confidence growing. 'I wouldn't want it for you either. But I do think you should appear on selected television shows, informing the public that you stand for quality and competitiveness. There's nothing like hearing the truth straight from the horse's mouth.'

'Thanks.'

'You're a handsome horse,' she said daringly.

'And one who prefers to remain in the stable!'

'We could find someone else within your organisation.'

He visibly relaxed. 'I can think of several who would be excellent. Elize Jordan for one. She heads our fashion-buying department, and is as decorative as she's intelligent.'

Abby knew instantly that the woman was important to him personally, though there was no indication of it in his voice. Indeed, it was the deliberately casual way he had spoken that had alerted her to his emotional involvement. It was a depressing realisation. Yet why should it be? She didn't even like the man!

'I'll see Miss Jordan at the first opportunity,' she said aloud.

'I've haven't yet agreed to ratify your contract.'

This was too much for Abby. How dared he encourage her to expound her ideas—even though many were the same as his—and then say he had no use for either her or her company? The man was an out and out sadist!

'There's nothing more to say until you've made up your mind what you want to do about us,' she stated, and again pushed back her chair.

'Sit down.'

It was a command, and hopeful that it meant an answer in the affirmative, she obeyed.

'One thing you'll have to learn when dealing with me,' he stated, 'is to control your temper.'

'The way you do?'

'I try,' he said cuttingly. 'Though I don't always succeed. But that's one of the perks of being top dog!' He managed a slight smile. 'I like most of your ideas and I'm prepared to implement them. Linking up the two different groups will take time and money, and it's important we don't lose our customers while we organise both. I look to you to promote a new, unified image.'

'What will the name be?'

'Coopers'.'

She lowered her eyes quickly, but not before he read the contents.

'No, Abby Stewart, I am not doing it out of ego, but because Henry suggested it.' He cleared his throat. 'When may I expect your proposals in writing?'

'Within twenty-four hours.'

'Make it twelve.'

'Impossible. I want to contact all the TV companies, and local radio stations around the country. I won't present you with pipe dreams, Mr Hunt.'

'Very well. You have twenty-four hours. Call my secretary and she will fit you in. Say it's Double "U".'

'W?'

'U.U. Utmost urgency.'

'I'd better remember that if I have to see you urgently at any time.'

'Use it unnecessarily, and it will be the last time you do.'

Dismayed by his flat tone—did the brute have no sense of humour?—she hastily apologised.

'I meant it as a joke, Mr Hunt.'

'*I* didn't. As you correctly pointed out, my time is valuable, and I can't afford to waste it.'

He reached for her coffee-cup but she shook her head.

'No, thanks,' she said. 'I don't want to keep you any longer. You promised me half an hour and I've already outstayed my welcome.'

He rose and pushed his hands deep into his pockets. 'I wonder what you'll be like at our next meeting?' he mused. 'First you were a clawing Kitten; now with your contract assured you're a cat that's swallowed the cream. Given your chameleon character, I shall have to ensure you don't become a man-eating tiger!'

He was the right one to talk about chameleons. His moods changed so quickly that it made her head spin. 'I don't think even a tiger would faze you, Mr Hunt. You probably keep a pith helmet and gun in your desk!'

'Now that's a suggestion I'll take up. Getting the last word with you won't be easy.'

'I'm glad we agree on something!'

'I hope we'll agree on many things, Miss Stewart, otherwise our working relationship will be extremely short.'

'On which happy note I'll depart,' Abby said coolly, and extended her hand. He enfolded it with his, the clasp firm but brief.

'Giorgio will see you out,' he said, resuming his seat and picking up *The Times* from a pile of dailies on the sideboard.

Well, she hadn't expected him to accompany her to the door, had she? She was working for him and should expect to be treated accordingly.

Elation at her success in securing the contract was marred by an inexplicable mood of irritation, further increased when she stepped outside the apartment block and saw a warden placing a parking ticket under the windscreen wiper of her car.

With a grimace of annoyance she plucked it off and stuffed it into her purse. Her breakfast with Rossiter Hunt had been an expensive one. She only hoped it proved worthwhile.

CHAPTER FIVE

CAROLINE looked up expectantly as Abby walked into the spacious open plan area of Stewart and Stewart's main office, and seeing the flash of her cousin's green eyes, followed her into her private office.

'How did the meeting go?' she asked.

'I'm still alive—just,' Abby retorted, flopping into the chair behind her desk.

Saying it aloud made her realise how close to the wind she had sailed. Though she always claimed never to find anyone intimidating, and knew she had performed well that morning—in spite of her initial shock at discovering Rossiter Hunt was the Rory she had encountered at the Kitty Club—she admitted that the man's exceptional dynamism had temporaily eroded her confidence.

It was a new experience and one she didn't enjoy— the more so since she knew it stemmed from her physical reaction to him. He was the last person she wanted to feel drawn to on that level, yet unfortunately her first sight of him the other night had intrigued her more than she cared to admit, and her second sight had confirmed it!

'You look as if you're sucking a lemon.' Caroline broke into her thoughts.

'Clever of you to guess!'

'You mean he didn't go for any of your suggestions?'

'Some he'd already thought of, and he appeared quite receptive to the others.'

'Then where's the problem?'

51

'It's the man himself. I didn't know until I saw him this morning that I had already met him.' She faced her cousin squarely. 'He was at the Kitty Club the other night with Kevin.'

Caroline was dumbfounded. 'You mean—you mean Rory and Rossiter Hunt are one and the same?'

'Exactly. You can imagine how *he* felt when he saw me and realised he had invited to breakfast a girl he had last seen dressed as a pussycat with a furry tail stuck on her behind!'

There was an astonished silence, then Caroline started to chuckle, the sound quickly turning into a gale of laughter.

For an instant Abby was furious, then she too saw the funny side of the situation and began laughing, her resentment against the man slowly lessening.

'I'm sorry,' Caroline said, regaining control of herself. 'I can see it must have been horribly embarrassing for you.'

'It was. And even worse when I explained I had been doing it to help you out, and he immediately informed me he doesn't want Kevin to become involved with you.'

'He actually said that?'

'Loud and clear.'

Caroline lowered her head, her hair falling over her face. 'I can't say I blame him. We've never met, but knowing I was a Kitten is a strike against me.'

'I agree. That's why I told him the reason you'd been working there. Not that it made any impact on him. He's as rigid as a wall, and once he makes up his mind about something he sticks to it.'

'Don't let it affect your relationship with him,' Caroline said quickly. 'He could be your biggest client.'

'I know. If it weren't for that, I'd tell him what he could do with his account.'

'Don't you dare! Anyway, you can put his mind at rest by letting him know I've no intention of seeing Kevin.' Caroline pushed her hair off her face and looked unusually determined. 'While I was at the club I had no choice, but he doesn't know where I live and none of the other girls will tell him.'

'But you liked him, didn't you?' Abby commented.

'Until I'm free I'm in no position to like anyone. All I want is to pull my weight here and then go home and take care of Charlie. I made such a mess of my life marrying Jeffrey, I'm scared of making the same mistake again.'

'Realising it was a mistake is halfway towards not repeating it,' Abby said gently. 'Once you're free of him you won't have any reason to hibernate. One day you'll remarry and Jeffrey will be a bad memory that will gradually fade. Not let's forget about him and get cracking on our campaign for Coopers'.'

Picking up a leather address book from her desk, she held it out to her cousin. 'Here's the listing of my contacts at the TV and radio stations, and national dailies. Beside each name is a list of the things they are interested in, so call those showing fashion, food, or personalities, and set up appointments with them.'

'All of them?'

'I doubt if more than ten per cent will show any interest,' Abby said drily. 'Rossiter Hunt may mean something to the financial Press, but apart from them he's a non-event. But with a couple of chat show interviews under his belt, everyone will be battling to get him.'

'Is he such an interesting speaker, then?'

'Yes.' Abby thought back to her meeting with him, and felt a little *frisson* shoot through her. 'He's also a grey-eyed Adonis with twice as much machismo!'

'Wow!'

'And a tongue like a knife.'

'A man not to be taken lightly,' Caroline added, and was half out of the door when Abby called her back.

'One other thing. Be an angel and call Rossiter Hunt's secretary and ask her to fit me in any time tomorrow. If there's a problem say it's U.U. —utmost urgency.'

'Yes, boss!'

Alone in her office, Abby swivelled round to her computer. But instead of turning it on, she stared pensively at the blank screen. Regardless of what she had said about the man she had just seen, he had made a more devastating impact on her than any other male she had met. In the space of less than an hour he had intrigued, aroused and infuriated her. Even worse, she knew with deadly certainty that he would go on doing so.

For the rest of the day she alternately typed furiously or sat back in her chair, deep in thought as she allowed concepts to flow into her mind and intuitively selected or rejected them.

So immersed was she that she was astonished when Caroline came in to say she was going home!

'So early?'

'It's five-thirty.'

Abby gaped at her. She recollected eating a sandwich and drinking endless cups of coffee, but had thought it was early afternoon.

'No wonder I feel exhausted,' she yawned, stretching her arms above her head. 'It's been a long, long day.'

'I made all the calls you asked me to do,' Caroline said, handing her a typed list of names. 'You underestimated Mr Hunt's appeal when you said we wouldn't get more than ten per cent interest in him. Every woman journalist and TV interviewer flipped at the offer of meeting him. He may have kept himself out of the limelight, but they all knew he was a rich, single, young dreamboat! Looks as if you can get him on any show or in any newspaper you want.'

'That's great. All I have to do now is make sure he doesn't bite any heads off!' Abby yawned again. 'What time am I seeing him tomorrow?'

'Ten-thirty.' Caroline glanced at her watch. 'I must dash. I have to collect Charlie from the crèche.'

'How is he settling there?'

'He loves it. You know he was the only good thing to come out of my marriage.' Caroline shook her head. 'I love being here with you—it's fun and exciting and I feel I'm learning a profession—but I hate being away from him all day. I feel I'm missing the best part of him. At least when I was at the club I was working evenings, when he was sleeping.'

Though deeply sorry for her cousin, Abby was hard put to it not to say her misfortune was of her own making.

'Once you learn the business,' she said instead, 'I'll see how good you are at writing promotional material. Then you could do quite a lot from home.'

'How fantastic! I——'

'Don't bank on it for the next few months. Until this new account is up and running, I'll want you here.'

Abby did not leave the office till midnight, but though she fell into bed the instant she arrived home, her sleep was restless and fitful.

At dawn she went for a jog round the block, finished off with a cold shower and, long before it was necessary, was dressed and ready to leave for her meeting. Deciding she might as well take advantage of her restlessness by arriving for it ahead of time and possibly chat to some of Coopers' personnel, she presented herself at Smallwood's an hour early.

The large, old-fashioned building situated on the Harrow Road was so unlike the image of Coopers' that she had difficulty envisaging Rossiter Hunt working here. It must have been a premonition, for when she gave her name and asked to be directed to his secretary's office the elderly receptionist looked at her in puzzlement.

'Mr Hunt? There's no one of that name here.'

'But I spoke to him here a few days ago—when I was with Mr Smallwood.'

'Oh!' Remembrance dawned. 'Mr *Hunt*. Of course. His joining us is so new that...' The woman smiled, shaking her head at the same time. 'But I'm afraid his office isn't here. It's at Coopers'. They're out on the North Circular Road. Shall I get you the address?'

Fuming, Abby nodded. She was mad at herself for not realising he wouldn't have had time to move in here, and madder with him for not having had the decency to tell her. Yet even as her anger with him mounted, she knew it was irrational. How was he to know she'd assume he was already at Smallwood's headquarters? The fact that Henry Smallwood's secretary, when asked to get Rossiter Hunt on the line, had only taken seconds to do so, hadn't meant he was in the same building. Dammit! One could be connected with Tokyo in five seconds flat. No, Abby admitted grudgingly, this mix-up was her fault entirely.

'Would you call Mr Hunt's secretary?' she asked. 'I have to speak to her urgently.'

'There are some house phones on the wall behind you. Pick one up and I'll connect you.'

Abby dashed over to the wall. A brief conversation with a Miss Pangrove ensued, the mistake explained, and the appointment switched forward a further half-hour, giving her ample time to get to her new destination.

Unfortunately, 'ample' didn't take into account the underpass being built on the North Circular Road, and the resultant traffic build-up moving at the pace of a one-legged tortoise, and she was fifteen minutes late when she arrived at the modern steel and glass office block, with the name COOPERS' emblazoned in brushed steel above the entrance.

Impatiently she waited to be taken to Miss Pangrove's office, and was flushed and anxious when she arrived there.

'I'm afraid Mr Hunt is with his next appointment.' Miss Pangrove, a gentle-voiced forty-year-old, gave her a sympathetic smile. 'I explained what had happened to you, and he said he'd see you as soon as possible.'

Abby had the feeling that 'as soon as possible' could mean six p.m.—she'd put nothing past him—and she rose and murmured she was going to make herself tidy.

In the well-appointed ladies' room she took several deep, calming breaths, repeating to herself that Rossiter Hunt had not deliberately misled her as to where he would see her. He had assumed her intelligence would make her realise that if he were 'taken over' on Thursday he'd hardly have time to move his entire operations within a week. No, the fault was hers. Yet why did she still blame him?

She had her answer an hour later when she was ushered into his office and saw the amused gleam in his eyes.

'Sorry to keep you waiting, Miss Stewart. I took it for granted you had Coopers' address.'

Odious man. He was rubbing salt on the wound. 'My fault entirely,' she trilled. 'But you're such a dynamo, I automatically assumed you'd be at Smallwood's the instant they bought you out and put you in command.'

The swift narrowing of his lids showed her she had scored a hit, but he fielded it straight back.

'Being in command, I commanded them to move *here*. This building is new, with the latest in technology, and there's ample space to absorb the staff we intend keeping.'

Determined not to continue this particular battle of wits, she crossed the wide expanse of charcoal-grey carpet towards him, confident that she looked feminine yet businesslike in a green and gold Max Liberati wool suit whose colour echoed the green of her eyes and the red-gold of her hair, and whose soft material moulded the fluid lines of her tall, slender body.

His office, different from his home, which was furnished with traditional elegance, was modern and functional in the extreme, with a bank of computer screens that she guessed would give instant access to the offices of his store managers. In such surroundings the man was far more impressive as he rose to greet her, and she was again acutely aware of the athletic physique that not even his sober charcoal suit could hide. She also noted that, like last time they had met, his pristine white shirt was twinned with a bright, hand-painted silk tie—a hint of less conventional depths beneath the surface conformity, perhaps?

'You must have a very varied workload,' he remarked, his eyes travelling over her as he waved her to a leather-backed chair in front of his desk, before resuming his seat.

'As varied as our plans for you,' she replied, making herself comfortable.

'Well, confound me with your brilliance.'

Silently she opened her Louis Vuitton briefcase, a present from a grateful client, and drew out two thick copies of a typed report. She handed one across to him, at the same time putting her briefcase on the floor. As she did, she accidentally over-stretched and his hand grasped hers instead of the folder. She pulled it back sharply, disconcerted by the tingle that raced through her body at his touch.

Confused, she fumbled slightly with the pages of her copy before beginning to read from them. Her voice, for a moment, seemed to come from a long way off, but she soon regained control of it and rattled off a variety of facts and figures before he interrupted her.

'I'm perfectly capable of reading the report myself, Miss Stewart. It will be quicker if I do and then discuss it with you afterwards.'

'When may I expect your call?'

'You won't be getting one.' Dark grey eyes met hers. 'Relax for ten minutes and I'll then give you my opinion. I did a speed reading course,' he added as he settled back in his chair and concentrated on the pages in front of him.

Apprehension flowed through her as she sat in silence. If he did not approve of the majority of the schemes she had put forward, he was ruthless enough to break their contract, and though they might manage to obtain a financial settlement, their being fired would be a talking point in the Press, and do their name no good.

Why, oh, why had she allowed his abrasive manner to make her lose her cool? If only their first sight of each other hadn't been at the Kitty Club! She writhed at the memory of her costume, knowing that every time she saw a fluffy pussycat tail she'd want to sink through the floor.

CHAPTER SIX

ROSSITER HUNT read the report quickly, and each time he turned a page, Abby noticed how nice his hands were: the fingers long and supple, the nails short and well-manicured.

Surreptitiously she shot a glance at her watch. It was fifteen minutes since he had begun, which meant he was thinking about each suggestion as well as reading it. Surely that augured well for her?

With a start she saw he had set the report on his desk and was leaning forward, hands clasped in front of him.

'You have some interesting concepts,' he said with grudging approval. 'I'm especially taken with your suggestion of introducing self-service restaurants into our larger stores, using only our own lines of food—was it your idea?'

'Yes. I'm so glad you agree with me!' She made no effort to hide her delight, and her eyes sparkled like bright emeralds. 'It would be relatively inexpensive to set up and run.'

'On the contrary. Doing it properly will be expensive, but it will greatly increase the sales of our pre-prepared meals.'

'Then you'll do it?'

'Eventually.' One dark eyebrow lifted. 'Unfortunately space is very tight, and until we open larger stores your idea is impractical.'

Abby felt she had been lifted to a great height and then dropped into a pit, and it took a moment for her to recover her equilibrium.

'Is this a habit of yours?' she muttered.

'Doing what?'

'Building someone up and then slapping them down.'

'Is that what you think I've done?'

She didn't answer, and he had the grace to look discomfited.

'I'm sorry,' he said so quietly she barely heard him.

'I beg your pardon?'

With the faintest of smiles he spoke more loudly. '*I'm sorry*. Did you hear that all right?'

'Yes, thank you, Mr Hunt. It wasn't too painful, was it?'

His mouth drew back to show his teeth. It wasn't quite a snarl, but it was definitely menacing.

'I think my main trouble with you, Miss Stewart, is that your Kitten image is still uppermost in my mind, and it's confusing the hell out of me.'

'Why?'

'Because I can't equate the intelligent woman you are with the fluffy-tailed girl I keep seeing in my mind's eye!'

Her cheeks burned. 'I've already explained why I was at the club, and it's unfair of you to keep referring to it.'

'It was your fluffy tail that intrigued me,' he ruminated, as if she hadn't spoken. 'And the special wiggle in your walk that made it bounce very sexily.'

Abby knew he was deliberately trying to rile her, and recognising that the least sign of temper would amuse him all the more, she gave a husky laugh and crossed her legs, allowing her skirt to rise above her knees and afford him a longer expanse of shapely leg on which to feast his eyes. If he insisted on seeing her as a sex object, she might as well use her assets to advantage!

'I always try to make the best of a situation,' she murmured, 'and when necessary I can do things quite out of character.'

'I'll bet.' His voice was deep and they gazed at each other in silence for a long moment.

'Regarding your suggestions for promoting *me*,' he said at last, 'I'm willing to be interviewed providing I approve of the interviewer, and the discussion is serious and well-balanced. But my private life has to remain private, and I won't answer any personal questions.'

'Fair enough,' Abby said, instantly curious to know something about it herself.

'As to your publicising anyone else in the organisation, I'm quite agreeable, as long as they are. I've spoken to Elize Jordan and she's quite taken with the idea. You should also see Enrico Salvini, the general manager of our food division. I'll call him and introduce you if he's around. He's young and handsome, and in my opinion highly promotional.'

Picking up one of the telephones on his outsize brushed steel desk, he asked his secretary to locate the man and send him in.

While they waited, Rossiter Hunt made no effort to speak, and Abby, intent on showing him two could play the same game, made a pretence of studying her report, though she knew it by heart. From the corner of her eye she saw him do the same, and as he lifted the pages towards him, a thin sheet of paper fluttered from between them to the ground.

Bending, he retrieved it. '"H.H.M.R.H."'?' he questioned, staring at the five letters repeatedly scrawled over the page.

Abby's heart missed a beat, but she managed to look unconcerned. 'Somebody's doodling,' she parried.

'*Yours*. Your writing is very distinctive.'

She peered at the paper. 'So it is. I often doodle when I'm thinking. It must have accidentally got caught between two other pages.'

'I'm not interested in how it got there, just what it means. R.H. are my initials, and I'm curious to know what H.H.M. stands for.'

Her heart missed another beat, but recognising he wouldn't let the matter drop, she decided on bluntness. 'It stands for His High and Mightiness.'

Without expression he regarded her. 'You find me autocratic?'

'Very.'

'Will it be a problem for you?'

Seeing the contract being torn up and her rudeness cited as the reason, she wished the floor would open and swallow her. If her father asked her to resign she wouldn't blame him. Somehow she had to minimise the damage.

'No matter how difficult the client,' she said, 'I've always managed to get along with them—even if I've had to eat humble pie—as I'm doing now! But I give of my best if I'm not on the defensive.'

'I had the impression you enjoyed a battle, Miss Stewart.'

'I do—if it's a fair one. But you're the client and therefore call the shots. So I can't fight you, can I? Leastways not if I want to retain your business.'

His jaw clenched and he frowned. 'Turning Coopers' around was damned hard and took all my energy, as well as a single-mindedness that brooked no argument—what you'd no doubt call high and mighty autocracy.'

'Too true! But as you are definitely top dog, don't you think the rest of the pack would work better if you didn't scare them to death?'

'Some of them have complained to you, have they?' he asked blandly.

'Of course not. I'm simply taking myself as an example.'

'Then don't.'

'Why not?'

'Because I've been different with *you*,' Rossiter Hunt said tersely. 'Tougher and sharper.'

'Why?'

'Blame our first meeting at the club.'

Abby gave a sigh of exasperation. She had already explained herself twice over and did not know what else to say.

'It won't happen again,' he went on. 'This report of yours shows initiative and intelligence, and I anticipate an amicable relationship with you. Business is tough enough as it is without having to protect my back in my own office.'

It took an instant for her to understand what he meant, then her cheeks flamed. 'Even if I thought you the most obnoxious person in the world, when I'm engaged by someone they have my total loyalty. And if I did want to stab you, Mr Hunt, it would be a full frontal assault!'

'Yes, I suppose it would. You're nothing if not honest, Abby.' His lids lowered, giving a calculating expression to his face, and she knew his use of her first name had been deliberate.

'I make your hackles rise, don't I?' he continued. 'And you do the same for mine. I wonder why?'

'Perhaps we're too similar.'

He snorted, any further answer forestalled by the entry of a slim young man in his middle thirties, with lustrous brown eyes, olive complexion and black curly hair.

'Ah, Enrico,' his employer said. 'I want to introduce you to Miss Stewart. Her company will be handling our public relations, and she may wish to enlist your help.'

'I am happy to do whatever I can.' With Continental gallantry, the Italian caught her hand and brought it to his lips, releasing it with great reluctance.

Abby was amused. Enrico Salvini was more akin to a soap-opera hero than head of the food department of a large chain. 'Highly promotional', Rossiter Hunt had called him, and she endorsed it—in spades! She immediately saw a hundred ways of presenting him to the public, particularly if he wasn't married!

Briefly she mentioned a few ideas, careful not to go into detail, and the Italian, determined to prove himself worthy of the part of media food expert, related one amusing anecdote after another concerning his work.

Glancing at Rossiter Hunt, she noticed his sour expression. What was bugging him? she wondered, intrigued when he suddenly cut across one of Enrico's stories.

'I don't think we need take any more of Miss Stewart's time, Enrico. I just wanted to make sure you are agreeable to do some publicity for us.'

'I'll do whatever is necessary,' came the enthusiastic reply. 'In fact I'd like to talk over a few things with Miss Stewart.'

Seeing he was about to launch into them here and now, she cut him short. 'It might be best if we meet on our own. How are you fixed for lunch some time soon?'

'Next week is terrible for me, but I can make myself available tomorrow.'

Abby frowned. She already had a lunch date, but had a feeling that to say no would not please the man behind her.

'Fine,' she replied, and about to name a restaurant, was forestalled by the Italian.

'Let me take you to Luigi's. It only has a dozen tables, but——' he kissed his fingers into the air '—it serves the best Tuscan food outside of Tuscany.'

'Sounds an interesting project for our food halls,' came Ross's acidic voice.

'My view entirely,' Enrico replied, oblivious of the sarcasm. 'I find inspiration everywhere—and most of all from beautiful women.'

Only when the door closed behind him, did the broad-shouldered figure at the desk speak again.

'Since Coopers' will inevitably be footing the bill for this gastronomic delight, please remember it's a working lunch, not a social one. Our accountants keep an eagle eye on the expense sheets.'

Flabbergasted by his remark, Abby silently counted to ten. 'I have a hearty appetite, Mr Hunt, and in case Enrico and I should talk generally and pleasantly for a few minutes, *my* company will gladly pay for the hors-d'oeuvres!'

She rose, a slight smile on her mouth as she saw the hard set of his. He rose too, his words cold as iced water.

'Don't worry about it, Miss Stewart. Look on your first course as a gift from me.'

'How generous of you. I'll make sure it's a pasta. I wouldn't want you to bankrupt yourself!' She glanced at her wristwatch. 'I'll have to fix an appointment with Miss Jordan some other time. I'm seeing another client in half an hour.'

'I'll tell her to expect your call.' Coming round his desk, he accompanied her to the door. 'Forgive me for not kissing your hand,' he said without expression as he opened it for her.

Not deigning to look at him she went to walk past, but before she could, a pocket Venus in her late twenties glided into the outer office. The woman was about five feet tall but exuded such vivacity she would never be lost in a crowd. Alabaster skin and classical features were highlighted by a full red mouth and bright brown eyes. Her hair, a cap of shining chestnut, was cut in a short bob, the sides slightly longer to curve forward on her cheeks.

'Elize!' Rossiter Hunt greeted her with a warm smile. 'You're just in time to meet our new PR representative.'

The warmth on Elize Jordan's face evaporated slightly as she gave Abby a quick head to toe appraisal.

'If you're going to promote the group,' she said in a voice that was surprisingly husky and deep for such a slender person, 'I hope you will start wearing our clothes.'

'It isn't part of our contract,' Abby answered gently, eyeing the woman's mulberry suit, its colour and cut doing wonders for the perfectly proportioned figure. No female had the right to be so tiny and yet voluptuous with it. It made Abby feel a clumsy giant; something she had never before experienced. 'I'd never have guessed *your* suit comes from Coopers',' she murmured.

'It's almost identical to one we're promoting,' came the reply.

'Really?'

'The only dissimilarity is that mine is in pure wool, and the buttons are leather instead of bone.'

'Such a small difference,' Abby said smoothly, and saw from the flash of the brown eyes that her innocent-sounding comment had been understood.

'I hope you two ladies will get together as soon as possible?' Ross spoke into the silence.

'I'm awfully busy,' Elize said. 'My only free time is eleven tomorrow.'

'I'll be here,' Abby accepted promptly and, realising that to allow the fashion buyer to irritate her would not be conducive to good working relations, hurriedly made amends. 'I intend promoting as many of Coopers' personnel as possible, and now I've had the pleasure of meeting you, Miss Jordan, I think you will be a marvellous asset.'

The coolness evaporated from the brown eyes and they sparkled with pleasure. 'I'll look forward to seeing you in the morning.'

Abby nodded, pleased with herself. Praise, however fulsome, never came amiss, and this dollop had scored a bull's eye. As she walked from the room, she was aware of Rossiter Hunt smiling warmly at Elize as he stepped aside for her to precede him into his office.

If that girl represented his taste in women, Abby thought sourly as she went down in the lift, it leaves me safe and sound! Not that she had any desire to be part of his personal life. She might find him physically attractive—heck, there was no might about it!—but she was darn sure they would clash in all other respects.

And yet...

Knowing she didn't appeal to him—except on the basest level, as his remark about her pussycat tail had signified—was unexpectedly depressing, and resolutely pushing personal thoughts from her mind, she went to her car.

Rossiter Hunt was her client. Nothing more.

CHAPTER SEVEN

ENTERING Elize Jordan's office next morning, Abby marvelled at how accurately it epitomised the woman's character—or at least the character she wished to portray!

Eggshell-blue walls and carpet, and an armchair and sofa covered with a Colefax and Fowler chintz in blue and peach, softened the hard edge of the functional teak desk and chair. Soft fabric and a rock-hard desk. The iron hand hidden by the velvet glove!

Settling into an easy chair opposite the sofa where Abby was sitting, Elize Jordan came instantly to the point.

'I'm intrigued to hear how you plan to promote the group, and also what you have in mind for *me*.'

Abby took a notepad and a sheaf of papers from her briefcase. 'Before we talk about promoting yourself, perhaps we should first discuss the new fashion image you will be projecting now you've merged with Smallwood's.'

'It has already been discussed internally.' Elize's tone was dismissive. 'We'll be adding a more sophisticated line for the thirty to fifties age group, and will design those departments accordingly.'

'How?'

'With mirrors, for one thing, and show-cases displaying our more expensive accessories like bags, shoes, belts. There will also be individual changing-rooms, thick carpeting, and chandeliers instead of halogen lighting.'

'Sounds great.'

'Of course I haven't discussed everything with Ross yet,' Elize went on. 'He's been too busy with the Smallwood's merger, but he——' she hesitated only momentarily '—he relies on me implicitly when it comes to fashion. In the four years I've been head buyer, our sales have increased dramatically each season.'

Elize would not lie—her assertion could too easily be checked—and Abby conceded that the woman was in an unassailable position.

'Now we are going up-market,' Elize continued, 'I'm certain my departments will contribute even greater profits to the group.'

'I believe Mr Hunt is also planning to cater for young children,' Abby declared, forbearing to say this was one of *her* suggestions.

'Really? He hasn't mentioned it to me.'

'It was a concept our company put forward,' Abby admitted, knowing that if she didn't, Rossiter Hunt was likely to do it for her.

'I see.' The small red mouth, with its very full lower lip, narrowed perceptibly. 'I assume you have market research to back up your proposal?'

'Of course. We also feel the children's and teenage departments should lead into one another.'

'Do you mean an identical sea of rails covering acres of open floor space? It will look as unexciting as a warehouse.'

'Not if the décor is different in each section.'

The older girl sat quietly, save for the rattle of her gold bracelets as she plucked at them with long scarlet fingernails. 'You aren't planning on joining Coopers', are you?'

Abby grinned. 'Hardly!'

'Then why are you extending your brief? I thought it was simply to get us the right sort of publicity.'

'When we take on a client,' Abby said, weighing her words carefully, 'we look to see if there are areas where what the client has to offer can be improved. As an example, if we handle a celebrity, we may suggest they have a different hairstyle or clothes to suit the image we're trying to project. We may even ask them to take up a specific cause or charity to will help widen their audience appeal.'

'What a phoney business you're in!'

'You could say the same of advertising agencies,' Abby retorted. 'Their business is to create demand, and so is ours. When we take on a company like this, we try to see ourselves as part of it—otherwise we'd remain detached and valueless.'

Elize rose and wandered over to the desk, delicately touching a crystal vase filled with pink roses, and slightly moving a large, silver-framed photograph of herself and Rossiter Hunt, smiling at each other. She glanced at Abby, one hand still on the frame, while the other smoothed her glossy chestnut hair.

'I appreciate the reasoning behind that, Miss Stewart, but please remember that I—and the buyers who work under me—have years of experience behind us, and will object to you coming on the scene telling us our business.'

'That isn't our intention. My company may suggest you cater for a different market, but we'd never advise you *what* to buy.'

'I'm not sure I agree about catering for young children. I'll talk it over with Ross tonight and——'

Elize stopped abruptly and took her hand from the photograph. She looked embarrassed, as if she had said too much, but Abby was convinced it was an act. The girl wanted her to know she was close to Rossiter Hunt apart from business hours, and was pretending she had let it slip accidentally. As if I care what they do in their spare time, Abby thought scornfully. All I'm concerned with is servicing this contract; I'll leave it to Elize to service *him*!

'Please don't think I'd use my personal relationship with Mr Hunt to undermine your position,' the older girl went on. 'You're studying us with fresh eyes and may well see things we have overlooked. But if I don't agree with you, I have to be honest about it.'

'Naturally.'

'I'm glad you understand. Now how do you envisage using *me* in your promotion?'

On safer ground, Abby launched into full flow. Having once had to promote a high-fashion boutique whose owner had been five foot ten and a hundred and eighty pounds, launching this sexy-looking pocket Venus was a doddle.

Abby felt as if she had been put through the wringer when she finally found herself on the other side of the office door. Elize Jordan might look fragile as a freesia, but she packed the same punch as her employer, and was someone to be treated with caution.

This was not going to be an easy account, she mused as she headed towards the lift, and the one thing she had to avoid was getting on the wrong side of a woman who had the boss's ear—among other things!

'Miss Stewart!'

The deep, incisive voice of the very man she was thinking about made her turn a startled gaze behind her, and she saw Rossiter Hunt beckoning her from the door of his office at the far end of the corridor. Pulses racing, she walked towards him.

He gave her an unexpected smile, his teeth strikingly white in his lean, tanned face. 'I've just had a word with Elize, and I'd like to have a word with you.'

'I'm meeting Mr Salvini in twenty minutes.'

'I won't keep you long.'

He waved her to a seat in a cushioned armchair away from his desk, and took one opposite.

'Elize says her discussion with you was very productive and that you both had some excellent ideas.'

Abby gave an involuntary smile, then hastily checked it, but he was too astute to miss it.

'No doubt each of you will claim responsibility for the best ideas!'

'If the stores do well, it will be credit enough for me,' she said flatly.

'Charmingly expressed.' His tone was mild though his look was searching, as if he wondered if any sarcasm was intended. However her calm air convinced him otherwise.

'Perhaps you'd like to appear on a chat show with Miss Jordan?' she ventured, playing him at his own game. 'If we could hint at a romantic connection it would generate marvellous publicity.'

'It would also generate your dismissal! I made my position clear last time we spoke, and I dislike having to repeat myself, so please listen carefully. *I will never discuss my personal life with anyone from the media.*'

'Sorry.' Abby was all sweet innocence. 'But you should understand that publicity has a habit of moving on its own momentum, and while I'll do all I can to follow your wishes, it may not be possible. As head of a high-profile group, you automatically arouse interest. It's part of the price you have to pay for success.'

'To a degree it's true, but just because my company has a high public profile it doesn't mean *I* have to have the same. There are many equally well-known businesses where you'd be hard pressed to name the chairman.'

He was right, of course, though she wasn't going to give him the pleasure of hearing her admit it.

'Cat got your tongue, Miss Stewart,' he asked pleasantly, 'or are you just a bad loser?'

'Neither. I simply have nothing further to say on the subject. Unlike you, I don't regard every discussion as a point-scoring competition!'

'Bravo! You wriggled out of that well. Now let's see if you can do the same with the next question. How did you enjoy your whirlwind visits to our stores the other night?'

It was impossible to hide her amazement. How had he known of it? Momentarily she was embarrassed, but almost at once it was overtaken by anger. He had no cause to make her feel sneaky when she had only been zealous.

'Do you take videos of everyone who goes into Coopers'?' she asked.

'My finding out was pure coincidence. Our underwear buyer happened to be at Smallwood's when you went there to see Henry, and he noticed you—what man wouldn't?'

Steely grey eyes locked with hers, and even across the width of the Lucite occasional table dividing them she felt the magnetic pull of them, and pressed her feet firmly on the ground in order to keep herself anchored there.

'He was doing some spot checks at half a dozen of our branches later that afternoon and evening,' the deep voice continued, 'and noticed you at four of them.'

'My going there wasn't a secret,' she shrugged. 'I wanted an up-to-date impression of your stores before preparing my report. I don't shop in them often enough to be familiar with them.'

He nodded, his dark chestnut hair catching the light. It was almost the same colour as Elize's, and she suddenly had an image of their two heads on a pillow. Hurriedly she blanked it out.

'I'd like to talk over some of the ideas you and Elize hatched,' he went on, 'but I know you're lunching with Enrico.'

'I can come back afterwards.'

'I won't be here. I'm driving to Manchester and staying overnight.' Lithely he rose and went to his desk. 'Trouble is I'm damn busy...' He frowned as he leafed through his diary. 'Do you object to a working dinner instead of breakfast?'

'Not at all.' Her tone was prim, hiding the unexpected surge of anticipation she felt at the prospect.

'Then let's make it tomorrow night at eight. I have a cancelled dinner engagement.'

Damn! Martin was taking her to see a rough cut of a film he had just directed, and would be hurt if she cried off.

'Can we make it another night, Mr Hunt? I've been invited to a film preview. A friend of mine has directed it and he——'

'Your boyfriend?'

Aware of her cheeks growing pink, she shook her head. 'Just a good friend.'

'That can mean nothing or everything,' Rossiter Hunt said silkily. 'But I suggest you explain to him that business has to come first—if you wish to retain it. I have no other night free in the near future.'

Abby would have given anything to see his diary, but accepting that he who paid the piper called the tune, she swallowed her indignation at his high-handedness, and nodded.

'Very well. Eight o'clock tomorrow night.'

'I'll collect you. Where do you live?'

'Highgate.'

'I'll either book somewhere nearby or in Hampstead, then.'

Abby left quickly, avoiding any comment from him, acid or otherwise, over her intended luncheon with Enrico.

The Italian was an amusing man, and only once—at the beginning of their meal—did she have to remind him that the purpose of their rendezvous was not to establish a personal friendship, but to ascertain how best he could publicise Coopers'.

He accepted the reprimand nobly, and was soon swamping her with a mass of projects. They were all interesting, and one was excellent.

'I'm a great cook,' he announced with no modesty, 'and can give demonstrations using the Italian products we sell. I could go from store to store and——'

'I'd like us to get a much bigger audience,' she intervened. 'Would you be nervous at cooking on TV? A producer I know wants a new cookery series, and I may be able to persuade him to do this one.'

'I'd love it.' Enrico puffed out of his chest. 'I will become a celebrity, yes?'

'Maybe,' she grinned. 'But I have to get the series accepted first.'

'I'm sure you'll succeed. You have the ring of confidence about you.'

'It's probably the toothpaste I use!' she quipped, and saw from his blank stare that he did not remember the famous advertisement she had often seen on TV as a child.

For the next hour they discussed various aspects of the series, and by the time she was in a cab on her way back to her office, Abby's hand was aching from the mass of notes she had scribbled down.

It was going to take effort to get this series on the air, but it had wonderful potential for Coopers' and would be a feather in her cap that could not fail to impress Rossiter Hunt.

And suddenly that was very important to her.

CHAPTER EIGHT

ABBY determined not to dress up for her dinner with Rossiter Hunt, but her decision was short-lived, and she donned a new Escada three-piece. The boxy wool jacket was the colour of the deepest violets, and trimmed with gold buttons at sleeves and pockets, matching the tiny buttons running down the front of the blush-pink pure silk blouse beneath, while a wide black leather belt circled her small waist, emphasising the fluid lines of the ankle-length flared skirt in a complementary violet and black dog-tooth check.

She applied more make-up than usual, lengthening and darkening eyelashes that had little need of additional artifice, deliberately exaggerating the size of her widely spaced eyes with violet shadow that emphasised their greenness, and drawing attention to her generously wide mouth with a glistening pink lipstick.

She experimented with various hairstyles, finally opting to keep it simple, and letting it fall, long and silky, to her shoulders. So must Delilah have looked when she had gone to seduce Samson, Abby mused, and though she reminded herself she was dining with a client, and one who was already involved with a woman, she was unable to dismiss the fanciful thought, which remained with her until the door buzzer rang at two minutes past eight.

Running to push the release catch, she wondered how to handle him if he spent the entire evening being rude and sarcastic. More easily than if he spent it flirting with her, she decided, and wasn't sure whether to say she was

coming down immediately, or invite him in for a drink. In the event, good manners won; they might be having a business dinner and not a social one, but there was no reason not to be well mannered—even if *he* wasn't!

'Would you care to come in for a drink?' she asked sweetly.

'Thanks.'

His tone gave away nothing, and irritated to find her heart beating fast, she opened the door and stood on the landing waiting for him, unable to contain her excitement as a firm tread came unhurriedly nearer.

'Hi!' she called, as he came into view.

It was the first time she had seen him in casual clothes, but the unstructured navy cashmere sports jacket, lighter blue trousers and cream silk polo neck suited his tall, athletic frame equally well.

'You look wonderful,' he said, his deep and sensuous voice sending a tingle along her spine.

'Thank you.' Leading the way into her living-room, she moved quickly towards the drinks tray on the narrow mahogany serving buffet standing behind a small, matching dining table. 'Wine or something short?' she questioned, aware of a faint tremor in her voice, and hoping he didn't notice it. 'We can talk business over it,' she added straightfaced.

'I'd say we're entitled to a non-working drink first,' he replied, his grey eyes silvering with amusement. 'I'll have a whisky.'

To her dismay conversation did not flow comfortably, for though *he* was at ease, she was unable to relax. What was the matter with her? Her parents often accused her of talking the hind leg off a donkey, and here she was *acting* like one! Yet for the life of her she found it impossible to make small talk.

'You're unusually quiet, Abby,' he commented, breaking a silence that seemed to have gone on forever.

His use of her first name confounded her all the more. Did he expect her to call him by his, or was he the sort of person who thought the hired help should not respond in kind?

'Perhaps you only sparkle during working hours?' he went on, cutting across her thoughts.

The bluntness of his question—in keeping with her knowledge of the man—did the trick, and she found her tongue. 'I don't find it easy making polite conversation with you.'

'Do you prefer us to argue?'

'We mainly do, don't we?'

His dark head tilted. 'I'd have said we strike interesting sparks off one another.'

'You might call it sparks, Mr Hunt, but I have the burns to show it was fire!'

'Make it Ross,' he flashed her a smile, 'and I promise to put salve on your wounds! In fact, if it will help heal the scars, I'm willing to treat this evening purely as pleasure.'

The leap of her pulses warned her not to accept the offer. 'I'd find it less of a problem if we didn't,' she managed to quip. 'Think how awkward it would be if I fell for your macho image!'

The grin that lit his face showed he hadn't taken her answer seriously, which was all to the good, for with deep foreboding she knew she had spoken the truth.

This man could mean more to her than a client!

Unconsciously she had recognised it during their first meeting, when his incisive intelligence and smouldering sexuality had sent her soaring into a mental high. But it had taken her till now to openly admit it, and with the admission came understanding of why she was knocking her brains out trying to devise the most brilliant promotional schemes of her career for him.

'Cat got your tongue?' he asked, breaking the silence.

No, she almost said, but *you* may be getting my heart. 'I've just realised I'm starving,' was what she said aloud.

'That's my cue, then.' He rose. 'I've booked a table at a new restaurant near here, and I've a feeling they'll give it to someone else if we're late.'

'I hate restaurants which do that,' she said as they went downstairs.

'Why? Empty tables mean lost revenue, and if you don't arrive on time they may label you a "no show".'

'I'd love to be a fly on the wall when *you* arrive at a restaurant and find your table's been given away!'

'If I'm going to be late, I call and let them know— one of the benefits of a mobile telephone!'

They reached the street and he opened the door of a sleek, dark Daimler, courteously waiting while she settled herself before moving round to take his place at the wheel. The polished wood and leather interior suited his powerful image, though to be honest she had expected him to drive something less stately.

To her horror she found she had verbalised her thoughts, and was relieved when he chuckled.

'In my twenties I had a Porsche,' he admitted, 'but I spent more time walking from my offices to the law courts than I did on the motorway, so I never had much chance to enjoy the power of it.'

'And now you have a different power, and don't need an outward one,' she commented, and saw him cast a quick glance at her.

'Not true, I'm afraid. When I visit friends in Germany I borrow a Lamborghini and let it rip!'

It was easy to envisage him doing it: long, supple fingers gripping the wheel, pugnacious jaw firm with concentration, thick chestnut hair tousled by the wind— he was certain to drive with the windows down!

With a start she saw they had reached the restaurant, and before she could step from the car he had come

around to open the door for her. It was an old-fashioned chivalry most men had discarded in the face of feminism, and showed another facet of his character. If she weren't careful she might find herself liking him as well as being sexually attracted to him!

'How does the décor strike you?' he murmured as they walked through the Grecian-style entrance to the restaurant.

'Painfully! But if the food's good, who cares?'

To her dismay they were shown to a table in the corner, alongside a wall. It was the best in the room, but it meant them sitting next to each other on a banquette, an intimacy she could happily have done without.

'Have you always lived in London?' she enquired, sliding into her seat and placing her bag between them.

'Enough to know I don't want to live anywhere else— except in the country.'

'Why don't you?'

'I may well do when I marry. It's the best place for children.'

'You sound as if you're already attached,' she said carefully.

'What a daunting word that is. Attached. Like a row of terraced houses!'

'How do you see marriage, then? As a detached house?'

He smiled, but seriously mulled over her question, his lower lip jutting forward. He had beautifully shaped lips, the top one narrow but humorous, the lower one fuller and sensual.

'I see marriage—my own, that is,' he said slowly, 'as a large house skilfully divided into two apartments. Not quite self-contained, but sufficiently so to give both owners room to do their own thing.'

Abby was disagreeably surprised. 'You mean you want an open marriage?'

'Certainly not. I just happen to believe every person needs their own space. I've been single too long to want to share every waking moment with my wife. Naturally that doesn't apply to my sleeping ones,' he added.

'Naturally,' Abby murmured, wondering why she had worried that she might grow to care for this man. He was an out-and-out pig!

'Want this?' he asked, holding out a knife.

'What for?'

'To cut me into little pieces! You almost felled me with one of your glances. They speak volumes, you know.'

Scarlet cheeked, she brazened it out. 'You have a vivid imagination, Mr—Ross. I don't know what you mean.'

'You disappoint me, Abby. I always believed you had the courage of your convictions. I've obviously said something to arouse your wrath, but if you won't tell me what it is, how can I apologise?'

'You wouldn't anyway.'

'Try me.'

She shrugged. 'It's your attitude to marriage. It seems terribly selfish.'

'Because I know what I want from it? As I'd only marry a woman with the same opinions as mine, the question of selfishness doesn't arise.'

'The same opinions on everything?'

'Yes.'

'How boring. If you always agree with each other, what will you have to talk about?'

'Not too much—which will suit me fine. I'm on my mettle twelve to fourteen hours a day, and when I came home I want to relax.'

'You'll be able to fall into a stupor!' she retorted.

He grinned. 'That won't happen to *your* husband, Abby. He'll probably run to his office for peace and quiet!'

'That's what my father says.'

'I think I'd get on well with him. We must meet some time.'

'You should anyway. He's head of the firm you've employed.'

'You're a director of it,' Ross commented. 'Have you always worked for him?'

Nepotism was the unspoken word, and she determined to scotch it.

'I cut my teeth with a rival company for a year, and then opened my own office. After I'd pitched for and won my father's biggest account, he made me an offer too good to refuse.'

'You're a tough lady.'

In his terms this was a compliment, but somehow she wasn't flattered. 'I'm not tough. I just want to be judged on ability. Dad saw me as his little girl, and learned the hard way that I was a chip off the old block.'

She picked up the menu the waiter had placed in front of her, suddenly hungry, which meant her earlier attack of nerves had gone.

When they had both given their orders and were sipping the excellent Montrachet Ross had chosen to complement their fish meal, he resumed his catechism, asking what other accounts she had handled, and how many she was working on now.

'Yours and Cartwrights'—the jewellers.'

His mouth narrowed. 'Are you behind the mass of publicity they've been getting lately?'

'Guilty,' she smiled.

'I hope we won't have to fight for your time?'

Abby's eyes sparked fire. 'I never take on more than I can handle, Mr Hunt.'

'Ross,' he corrected.

'If you intend to go on attacking me, I'd rather it was Mr Hunt.'

'Ross,' he repeated. 'And I apologise.'

Their first course arrived, and Abby concentrated on the poached scallops as if they were diamonds.

'Stop sulking,' he said. 'I've apologised and I meant it.' He refilled her wine glass. 'The idea for that cookery series for Enrico is great. If you get it on television I'll give you a bonus.'

'Not necessary, thanks.'

'When will you know if you can get it on the air?'

'I spoke to a production company this afternoon, and they said it's exactly what they're looking for.' His astonishment was gratifying, and she basked in it. 'I have another idea for you to consider.'

'I'm all ears,' he said indulgently.

She had removed her jacket when they sat down, and she was conscious of his eyes lowering to her neckline. Automatically her hand went to the top button of her blouse to make sure it had not come undone and, as if realising what her gesture meant, a slight smile quirked the corners of his mouth.

'All eyes would be a better metaphor!' she responded coolly.

'If you dress to attract, don't blame me for noticing.'

'I dress to please myself,' she snapped. 'But if we ever have to spend another working evening together, I'll wear a shroud!'

'I suspect you'd even look sexy in that!' His gaze ranged over her. 'Do you have a boyfriend?'

'Several.'

'No one special?'

'No.'

'You surprise me. You're very pretty and very bright.'

'*You're* very handsome and very rich. Why aren't *you* married?'

'I'm considering it.'

Abby was surprised by the dismay she felt. Though Elize had subtly warned her Ross was out of bounds, she had not entirely believed her. Now it appeared she was wrong.

'Won't Elize object to you flirting with me?' she questioned bluntly.

'Are you planning to tell her?'

'Snitching is not my style.'

'I'm glad to hear it.' He waited in silence till the waiter had removed their plates. 'Surely many clients have fancied you?' he asked when they were alone again.

'True, but they took "no" for an answer.'

'I haven't heard you say "no".'

'I thought it was obvious. I don't date men who have girlfriends.'

'I was under the impression most normal bachelors have them!'

He turned to face her directly, and the movement brought his knee into contact with hers. Quickly she drew back, and if he noticed he gave no sign of it.

'Tell me about your childhood,' he went on conversationally. 'It may help me to understand why you haven't succumbed to my charms like every other female!'

He was openly laughing at her, she knew, but she refused to rise to the bait.

'I had a very happy childhood,' she said primly. 'I have no brothers or sisters, but was brought up with Caroline when her parents were killed. I'm close to my parents and can talk to them about everything.'

'What did they think of your stint at the Kitty Club?'

'Hardly a stint,' she said irritably. 'I was there for one night as a favour to Caroline, so do you mind not referring to it again? The joke's wearing thin.'

'Point taken. But do go on.'

'I've finished. Now it's your turn to tell me about *your* childhood. It may help me to understand why you're a sex maniac!'

'*Touché*!' he chuckled. 'But I'm afraid it won't give you a clue. I was as happy as a child as you were. I have two younger sisters, both married, and my father was a judge—hence my original interest in the law. We were comfortably off, but my uncle was the only seriously rich member of the family. He and his wife unfortunately had no children, and doted on us. Hence my good fortune today.'

His modesty pleased her. 'You earned it, Ross. You did a great job turning the company around. Without you, it would have gone bankrupt.'

'You're exaggerating—but my mother would adore you!' His expression grew tender. 'Until she retired she was a social worker; the kind who cares deeply for everyone.'

'As I care for my clients!'

His mouth tilted upwards. 'Except that their troubles are probably less intractable. As a last resort you can always tell them to go to hell.'

'I'm giving serious thought to doing that with someone at the moment!'

'Anyone I know?' he asked with mock innocence.

'It isn't ethical for me reveal his name,' she said poker-faced.

'If I guess correctly do I get a sweet and a kiss?'

Unable to stop herself, she burst out laughing and he joined in.

'This has been a most enjoyable evening,' he said soberly after a moment—though amusement still curved his lips. 'I hope you'll come out with me again.'

An image of Elize prevented her saying yes, and without answering him she plunged her spoon into the chocolate-covered profiteroles she had ordered, and took a mouthful.

'So far I have always got what I wanted,' he said softly. 'Remember that, Abby.'

'I'll write it down and hang it above my bed.' Even as she spoke she knew she had said the wrong thing, and she went scarlet with embarrassment as he gave a wicked chuckle. But he was gentleman enough to change the subject.

'One other thing I've learned about you,' he went on, 'is that you enjoy eating. I get irritated by women who peck at their food.'

'No fear of that with me. The meal was delicious.'

'I agree. I'm surprised the place is only half full.'

'They need our firm to promote them.'

'I'll let you know if I agree with *that* when I see what you've done for mine.'

'Still have no faith in my talents?' Mellowed with the golden Montrachet, she wasn't aware how seductive her voice sounded until she saw he was staring at the soft fullness of her mouth.

'It depends which talents you mean.' He slid closer along the seat, and because she was against a side wall she was unable to move away from him.

'Not the obvious ones,' she murmured, refusing to look at him.

His fingers played delicately on her arm, sending a wave of languor through her body. 'I suspect hidden depths, and I'm looking forward to exploring them.'

The image of Elize was too strong for Abby to enjoy this sexual word-play, and all she felt was anger. Forcibly reminding herself that Ross was a valuable client, she spoke in dulcet tones.

'It would be better if we waited until you were no longer a client before we think in personal terms.'

'A very tactful brush-off,' he said silkily, drawing away from her. 'I've never been turned down with such expertise.'

'I'm surprised you've *ever* been turned down,' she smiled, attempting to make light of it.

'I was fourteen at the time, and going through a spotty stage!'

Relieved by his humour, she lost her tension. Rejecting a man was embarrassing at the best of times, but in a case such as this it could mean losing the account if it wasn't done diplomatically.

Over several cups of coffee, she encouraged Ross to air his own ideas for promoting the stores, and it was midnight before the Daimler drew to a stop outside the block where she lived, and Ross accompanied her to her front door.

Nervously she wondered if, in spite of her rejection, he would suggest coming in for another coffee, and she was considering what to do if he suggested it when he spoke.

'We've had a successful evening—businesswise!' he said drily. 'Tomorrow we'll start putting into action some of the things we've discussed.'

She nodded and unlocked her door, her relief dying as he stepped inside and caught hold of her, effortlessly swinging her round to face him.

Before she had a chance to pull free, his mouth came crushing down on hers. It was warm and firm, as were the hands that moved along her spine to cup her buttocks, drawing her closer to the hardness of his thighs. She was alive to the heat radiating from him, and breathed in the spicy scent of his aftershave and the disturbing scent of the man himself. It reminded her of pine trees and warm sunshine; of fireflies and candlelight.

Her thoughts were as confused as her emotions, but as his warm tongue snaked between her lips, reason dissolved and she abandoned all attempt to remain detached. Her head tipped back and every limb trembled, the innermost part of her pulsating with a surge of desire that left her weak with longing. The strength of her arousal frightened her, for desires had been released which, even if she denied them, would not lightly be dismissed. Yet she dared not give in to him. To do so was a total negation of her principles.

Fortunately she had no need to wrestle with them further, for as suddenly as he had caught hold of her, he let her go.

'That was a sample,' he said thickly, lifting his hand to brush back a dark strand of hair from his forehead. 'I'll save the best for later.'

He turned and, without a backward glance, strode away.

It had all happened so fast that, by the time she had double locked the door and crossed the entrance hall to her bedroom, she began to doubt it had taken place. But the hot imprint of his lips still lingered, and she was astonished by the quiver that surged through her as she recalled his touch.

But as she prepared for bed she also recalled his parting words. How conceited he was, how arrogant, how *experienced*! He had read her mood completely; had known that despite the brush-off she had given him in the restaurant, she wanted him as much as he wanted her. The only trouble was that if she gave in to her feelings, her wanting was likely to outlast his.

And there was still Elize. Whatever integrity Ross displayed in his business affairs, he had none when it came to women. Bitterly she regarded herself in the bathroom mirror. Her red-gold hair fell to her shoulders in soft, bouncy waves, and her face glowed like a dew-kissed rose. She looked beautiful and sexy and ripe for the taking. And that was all Ross saw when he looked at her. For that reason, if for no other, she must never give in to him, for he could break her heart and walk away without regret.

CHAPTER NINE

THE crisp winter air, lit with bright sunshine, matched Abby's happy mood, and added a rosy glow to her already animated features as she moved jauntily along the street and entered Coopers' building.

Two middle-aged men stood aside as she slipped into the waiting lift, and she was conscious of their admiring glances. In a striking yellow and black serape over a high-necked yellow wool dress, belted in wide black leather, she looked sensational and knew it. She only hoped Ross agreed.

Of course he might not be here. After all, it was Elize she had come to see this morning. Still, if he was in, she would ask his secretary if he had a few minutes free. If he did, she could always find something to ask him!

'Hi.' Elize was waiting to take the lift as Abby stepped from it, and greeted her with a smile. 'Go right ahead to my office, I'll be with you in a minute.' Eyes sharp as a whippet slashed her, causing a sensation of discomfort. 'Introduce yourself to my baby brother,' the girl added as the door closed on her.

Abby imperceptibly paused as she passed the door leading to Ross's suite, but she quickened her step almost immediately. How embarrassing if he came out and found her standing there!

Arriving at Elize's office, she pushed open the door and entered, fully expecting to see a small boy. But the only person there was six feet tall, several years older than herself, and was someone she had already met.

'Kevin!' she cried in astonishment.

'My God!' His surprise echoed hers. 'Carla's friend—
how fantastic. Don't tell me my sister's hiring Kittens to
parade round the fashion departments!'

'Hardly,' Abby grinned. 'I'm the new PR for the
group. I was a Kitten for one night only, to help Caro—
Carla,' she corrected herself. 'I'm her cousin.'

'I see,' he said slowly. 'I was pleased to hear she'd
found another job, but the club refused to tell me where
she went or where she lives. It's a real stroke of luck
meeting you like this. Now you can give me her address.'

'I'm afraid I can't. She has some personal problems
to deal with, and doesn't want anyone to know where
she is at the moment.'

'Maybe I can help with her problems? If she's in
trouble—— '

'She isn't. She simply wants to be left alone.'

Kevin half turned away, giving Abby the opportunity
of studying him. There was little family resemblance between him and his sister, other than their both having
fair skin and brown eyes, for he was tall, with light brown
hair and unremarkable features. But the most obvious
difference was his air of gentleness, which was completely at variance with Elize's vivacious manner.

'You almost called her Caroline,' he said unexpectedly. 'Is that her real name?'

'Yes.'

'I'm going to find her, you know. As soon as I met
her, I knew she was going to be important to me. I can't
get her out of my mind.'

'That's understandable. She's very pretty.'

'It's more than the way she looks; it's the way she is.
Vulnerable and innocent.'

Well, he had got that right, Abby thought, giving him
full marks for character assessment. But she was still
reluctant to break her word to Caroline, who did not

want to become involved with anyone until she was legally free of Jeffrey.

'I must see her,' Kevin reiterated. 'I won't tell Rory or my sister it was you who gave me her address, so you've no worry on that score.'

'What does Ross have to do with it?' Abby questioned curiously.

'He and Elize are very close—our families have been friends for years—and she was the one who persuaded him to come to the club with me and meet Carla—Caroline—for himself. But you know all that, don't you? I still cringe when I remember how rude he was to you.'

'Better me than Caroline,' Abby retorted. 'If he'd said half the things to her that he did to me, she'd have burst into tears.'

'Which proves my point that she's vulnerable,' Kevin said swiftly. 'Won't you let me see if I can help solve her problems?'

'I'll tell her what you've said, but I honestly feel you should take your family's advice and forget her.'

'I'm not a child who doesn't know its own mind,' he protested angrily. 'If you——' He broke off as his sister came in.

'Really, Kevin, why didn't you offer Abby a coffee?'

'Sorry, Liz. I forgot.'

'I don't want one anyway,' Abby placated.

'That isn't the point.' The scarlet lips thinned. 'There's a right and wrong way to behave.'

Kevin flushed, and Abby recalled his saying he wasn't a child, though it was clear his sister still treated him as one. If the rest of his family behaved the same, no wonder he was lacking in confidence. It also gave her a clue as to why he had fallen for Caroline. Her vulnerability obviously made him appear strong.

'I'll push off,' he said, and gave Abby a smile as he left.

She returned it, ruefully conceding she hadn't heard the last of him. Aware of Elize watching her, she said the first thing that came into her head.

'You told me your kid brother was in here, and I expected to meet a schoolboy!'

'Occasionally he acts like one, though in business he's amazingly astute. He's manager of one of our main stores and is destined for great things. It's only in his personal life that he's a fool. Some little gold-digger thought she'd hooked him, but I think Ross has frightened her off.'

Abby stayed silent. Evidently Ross hadn't told his ladyfriend of her own connection with Caroline, and she saw no reason why *she* should. To avoid further discussion of Kevin and his private life, she opened her briefcase and extracted the notes she had written.

For the next hour they discussed her proposals for promoting the fashion department, and Elize agreed so easily to all of them that Abby wondered at this sudden subservience. It somehow seemed out of character.

'What do you have lined up for Ross—Mr Hunt?' the girl asked.

'Various newspaper interviews, and several TV chat shows. Gary Winton's very keen and has given me three dates when he can have him on his programme. I'll need Ross to tell me *his* available dates.' Intentionally she used his first name. He had asked her to do so, and she was irritated by the way Elize tried to show her closeness to him.

'Ross can't stand that man,' Elize said.

'One doesn't have to like him personally,' Abby pointed out. 'The important thing to remember is that Gary draws ten million viewers.'

'I'll tell him all you've said. If *I* can't get him to change his mind, no one can.'

The purring satisfaction in the husky voice was more than Abby could tolerate, and she rose to leave. As she did, the door opened and in came the man they had been discussing.

He dwarfed the room with his size, yet he moved with the sleek grace of a panther. A panther ready for the hunt this morning, if the sharpness in the grey eyes was anything to go by.

'Before you leave, Abby, I'd like a word with you in my office,' he rasped.

She hid her surprise. No hello, no smile, no social chit chat of any kind, just an order. After his parting kiss yesterday, she had expected something less impersonal.

'I'm afraid I don't have the time,' she replied coolly.

'Make it.'

His authoritative tone left no room for arguing, and with a shrug of resignation she picked up her briefcase.

'Go on ahead,' Ross instructed her. 'I just want to have a word with Elize.'

Abby stormed down the corridor to his room and flung her things on to the nearest chair. No client had ever treated her so rudely; he really was the most arrogant man she had met. How long did he intend to keep her waiting? she wondered, and decided to give him ten minutes. If he hadn't returned by then, she would leave and damn the consequences.

No sooner had she decided this than she heard the door open, and she pretended to be absorbed in a large Hockney painting that almost covered half a wall. It was of the artist and some friends grouped around his California swimming-pool, and carried a strong feel of summer.

'Are you an admirer too?' Ross asked behind her.

'Yes,' she answered shortly, refusing to look round at him.

to go by, Caroline will be the one to suffer. He appears to have a low level of boredom.'

'That's often the case until the right woman comes along,' Abby said coolly, and closed the door swiftly behind her, giving him no chance to make any further comment.

When she arrived back at her office, Caroline took one look at her and shook her head. 'I don't know what gives at Coopers' but you always return from there looking ready to kill someone.'

'I am—Rossiter Hunt.' Abby dropped into her swivel chair and furiously spun it. 'I bumped into Kevin when I was there,' she said as it came to a stop, and briefly recounted the morning's events. 'Do you want me to give him your phone number or not?' she finished.

'Absolutely not. If you do, you can kiss Coopers' goodbye.'

'Don't let that govern your decision,' Abby stated. 'We managed very well without it, and——'

'The answer's still "no". Anyway, it's best if I don't start dating till I'm free of Jeffrey. If Kevin's interested in me six months from now, I'll consider it. By then you'll be so enmeshed in Coopers', Horrible Hunt won't find it easy to fire you!'

Abby's relief that she didn't have to put Ross to the test at this precise moment was short-lived, for two days later Kevin came to see her.

'Forgive me barging in on you,' he began as he was shown into her room, 'but I want you to give Caroline this.' He placed a sealed envelope on the desk. 'I've written saying how much I want to see her and—well, I'm hoping that after she's read this she'll change her mind and meet me.'

'You're certainly persistent,' Abby remarked, wishing Ross were the same.

'I haven't always been,' he admitted. 'That's why Elize and Rory don't take my feelings for her seriously.'

Abby's heart thumped. 'Your sister knows of my relationship to Caroline?'

'Rory told her.'

'I bet she wasn't overjoyed!'

'She wanted him to fire you!' Kevin's face flamed and he groaned. 'Hell! I shouldn't have told you that. Still, you don't have to worry; Rory refused.'

'Good for him,' Abby said sarcastically. 'I like a man who knows his mind.'

'Then you must be crazy over Rory! Even if he'd wanted to dispense with your services, the minute Elize insisted he did, he dug his heels in and said no.'

Abby had never thought Elize would earn her undying gratitude, which went to show one should never assume anything! Bolstered by all she had just learned, she dialled the number of her cousin's intercom. 'Please come in right away?' she said, and hurriedly set down the receiver.

'Will you give my letter to Caroline?' Kevin reiterated.

'You can do it yourself,' Abby replied as the door opened and the girl came in.

The look of pleasure on both their faces as they greeted each other convinced her this was more than a passing fancy for either of them, and tactfully murmuring she would be back in ten minutes, she left them alone.

When she returned, Kevin had gone, and Caroline was luminous with joy.

'I'm so glad he refused to take no for an answer,' she cried. 'I'm having dinner with him tonight.'

'I thought you didn't want to date anyone in case Jeffrey found out and caused trouble?' Abby couldn't help saying.

'I told Kevin about him—and also that I have a baby— and he said I was worrying for nothing—that Jeffrey had walked out on *me* and I could divorce him no matter how many men I dated.'

So all's well that ends well, Abby mused as Caroline waltzed out. If only her own love life were as easily resolved! Why wasn't Ross short and fat instead of a dreamboat? Better still, why wasn't Elize short and fat? Then Ross would have been free and she herself would have had no reason not to go out with him.

Frowning, she swivelled in her chair. Who was she fooling? If there had been no pocket-sized Venus in his life there would have been some other girl. And even if not, his blueprint for a happy marriage didn't make him husband material. Leastways not *her* husband.

'So keep reminding yourself how unsuitable he is, and forget him!' she muttered, and swivelling round to her computer, concentrated on her workload.

At the end of the week she went to see Enrico. A TV company had commissioned the cookery series and deputed her to decide what part the Italian should play in it. She had not been to Coopers' since her last angry meeting with Ross, and though—courtesy of Kevin—she knew she wasn't going to be fired, she was pretty sure Ross intended to give her a hard time. If only he were abroad for a few months! By then he would realise how happy Kevin and Caroline were together.

But it was not to be. As she passed the reception desk on her way out, after a productive hour with Enrico, the girl on duty said Mr Hunt had called down to say he wished to see her before she left.

He was standing by his desk as she entered his room, and instantly came to the point.

'I hear Kevin went out with your cousin. I think you owe me an explanation.'

Seeing the lean, handsome face glowering at her, Abby mentally prepared to do battle.

'He came to my office and asked me to deliver a letter to Caroline, and it seemed childish to keep them apart. After all, they aren't children.'

'You deliberately ignored my order.'

'I felt it wasn't your business to issue orders to me on a personal matter. Kevin seems fond of Caroline, and she of him.'

'*Seems* being the operative word,' he said scathingly. 'He's fallen in love five times in as many years, and I can't see this one being any more durable.'

'Maybe they won't be. But that still doesn't give you the right to vet whom he sees. You act as if he's a half-brained adolescent.'

'Emotionally he is!'

'It's still not your concern. He has to grow up some time, and if you're always acting the guardian, what chance does he have?'

Painfully aware of Ross's thunderous expression, Abby picked up her briefcase from the floor, but not wanting to leave on a sour note, attempted to reason with him. 'Why not meet Caroline? I'm sure you'll feel differently once you get to know her. She really isn't as you imagine.'

'That applies to most women,' he said drily, 'and particularly you.'

Abby knew he was not being complimentary, but didn't bother arguing the point.

'Is that a "yes" or a "no"?' she said instead.

'It's an "I'll think it over",' he replied flatly, and lapsed into silence.

Assuming the interview was over, she turned to leave, but was stopped by a lift of his hand.

'Given your obvious dislike of me, Abby, don't you feel it might be better if your father took over from you here?'

Her heart sank. It was tantamount to being fired, and she knew her father would be upset she had allowed personal feelings to come between herself and a client.

'At least you aren't denying your dislike,' he said drily.

'Don't put words into my mouth.'

'I wouldn't dream of it. You usually have more than enough to say for yourself!'

'I'll remember to be docile when I'm with you.'

'You'd never succeed.'

'Don't bet on it,' she flared.

'Why not? I like the occasional gamble—so let's see if I'm right.'

Before she knew what was happening, his arms snaked out and pulled her hard against him, his fingers biting into her arms like iron clamps from which there was no escape. At the same time his mouth covered hers, his tongue forcing her lips open and searching the inner softness with a warm, searching intimacy.

Despite her assertion that she was capable of being docile with him, her instinct was to struggle. How dared he kiss her with such passion when he was romantically linked with another woman? Didn't he have any shame? Forcing herself to remain motionless, she tried to ignore the feel of his plundering tongue, and had almost reached the end of her control when he seemed to realise she wasn't putting up the fight he had expected.

With a husky murmur his tight hold decreased, though he still held her close as he withdrew his tongue and gently licked her lips. His gentleness was her undoing and desire trembled through her, permeating every nerve in her body. With a soft cry she wound her arms round his neck and gave herself up to his kiss, her lips parting to let him penetrate her again. The throbbing pressure of his body showed all too clearly what her response was doing to him, and her desire increased, coursing through her body to settle into a yearning ache between her thighs.

'Ross,' she whispered against his mouth. 'Oh, Ross——'

With a suddenness that shocked her, he relaxed his grip on her and stepped back. A flush lay on his high cheekbones and the glitter of passion darkened his grey eyes, but the expression on his face was mocking.

'Looks as if I've lost my gamble.' His voice was still husky but controlled. 'You passed my test with flying colours.'

Humiliated by the shabby trick he had played on her, Abby tried to stay calm, but every nerve in her was still quivering with desire and frustration—as much as fury at the speed with which he had regained his equilibrium—and it made it difficult for her not to explode with anger. But she would die rather than give him the satisfaction of knowing the passionate emotion he had aroused in her.

'Don't experiment with me again, Ross. There's a limit to what I'll accept—even to keep an account as important as yours.' Abby marvelled at her ability to speak so calmly. 'Now if that's all...'

Again she turned to leave, and he made no move to stop her.

'I'll give you my decision about meeting your cousin when I see you again,' he said as she reached the door.

'Fine,' she replied without bothering to look at him. Then, resisting the urge to slam the door, she closed it very softly.

Only then did she give free reign to her anger. Storming down the corridor, she silently reviled Ross, calling him every name she knew, and some she hadn't even realised were in her vocabulary!

The manner in which he had humbled her was despicable and ruthless, and she wished she had the freedom to tell him to go to hell! But her father was the senior partner and it was not her decision to make, added to which the most humiliating aspect of the whole affair was that even if she no longer wanted the Coopers' account, today had conclusively proved that she *did* want Ross Hunt.

CHAPTER TEN

'YOU'RE turning into a workaholic,' Arthur Stewart chastised his daughter as he popped his head round her office door.

She was seated at her desk, absorbed in documents, her shoulder length red-gold hair piled roughly on top of her head, giving her the appearance of a wayward nymph.

'It's eight o'clock and you should be out enjoying yourself,' he continued. 'And if you don't have a date, you should be at home relaxing. Caroline's complaining you're driving yourself too hard.'

Sweet Caroline, Abby thought. Her cousin was so grateful to her for giving her a job and bringing Kevin back into her life that she had started worrying over her like a mother hen with her chick. She wondered suddenly how the romance was progressing. She had been so busy lately there had been little time to chat, though she knew they were seeing each other regularly. If Ross was aware of it, he must be furious.

'Care to have dinner with us?' her father questioned. 'Knowing your mother, I'm sure she's cooked enough to feed an extra six!'

'Thanks, but I'm too tired. A hot bath and bed is what I need.'

'And food,' was her father's parting comment.

Abby knew his concern was well founded. Determined not to let her personal dislike for Ross influence her, she had worked like a demon these past three weeks, and her enterprise had been rewarded with two excellent television interviews with Elize and Enrico, as well as a mass of newspaper coverage. But still bruised by her last encounter with Ross, she had not yet started working on his promotion.

Closing her slim Cross biro, she stretched her arms lazily above her head and then, removing the few pins that held her hair, let its rich wealth tumble carelessly on to her shoulders. It was time to go. Her head was aching and she was no longer thinking clearly.

Entering her flat, she heard the cheerful mewing of Genghis, her black Persian cat, and lifting him up to cuddle him, she went into the kitchen.

She was longing for a drink, and after placing a frozen chicken casserole in the microwave to defrost, opened the refrigerator and took out a half-full bottle of New Zealand Chardonnay.

About to flop on to the settee in the living-room, she set down her glass and went into her bedroom to change into a fluffy jade angora dressing-gown, a colour that almost matched her eyes. Her mother had bought it for her, and though no longer fashionable or new, it was cosy and comfortable and perfect for an evening alone.

Curling up against the cushions, she sipped her wine and felt the day's tension drain away. All she needed now was some music. Reaching to the fitted bookcase behind her, she slipped a disc into the CD and allowed the soft strains of the Brahms Piano Concerto to lull her into a half-sleep.

Barely had the second movement started when the bell rang. It was probably Ann, a friend who lived nearby and often dropped in unannounced. A neighbour must have come in at the same time, for she hadn't pressed the entry-phone.

Glass in hand, she opened the front door, nearly spilling her wine as, instead of Ann's slender figure, she saw the tall, broad-shouldered one of Ross Hunt.

In another of his impeccably tailored charcoal pin-striped business suits, worn this time with a burgundy and white striped shirt, and solid burgundy tie, he was every bit as devastating as she remembered. His hair was ruffled as though wind-blown, and because it fell forward, a few chestnut strands were visible among the near black hair. Inexplicably she felt the need to touch it, and was instantly furious with herself.

'What do you want?' she questioned.

'To come in for a start.'

Ungraciously she ushered him into the lounge. A soft fold of angora wool caught between her bare legs, and she would have tripped had not two strong hands come out to steady her.

'How many glasses have you had?' he asked.

'I'm not drunk, if that's what you're implying. My dressing-gown's too long if I don't wear slippers.'

'Then why don't you?'

'I enjoy the feel of carpet under my feet.' She inched back from him. 'Would you care for a drink?'

'No, thanks. But don't let me stop you.'

'I'll have a second glass with my dinner. I haven't eaten yet.'

'I shan't keep you from it long,' he said, taking the hint, and sat down in an armchair.

It was difficult to fathom his mood, save that it was not particularly friendly. Perhaps he had come to thank her for her efforts on behalf of his company. On her recent visits to Coopers' he had either been absent or chosen not to see her, and though other members of his staff had praised her, no word had come from him.

She sat down and reached for her glass. As she did, her dressing-gown slipped open, exposing her legs almost to the top of her thighs. Hurriedly she wrapped the jade wool around her and tightened the belt, but not before she had seen his eyes riveted on her naked flesh.

'You have beautiful legs,' he commented matter-of-factly. 'It's a pity to hide them.'

'I don't when I'm on the beach.'

Disconcertingly his eyes ranged slowly over her, as if itemising every part of her anatomy.

'Why are you here?' she demanded. 'I assume it's something important?'

'It's about your bloody cousin!' His voice was harsh. 'She tried to milk Kevin for money, and I want you to inform her that if she does it again, I'll go to the police.'

Indignantly Abby jumped to her feet. 'Caroline's the least mercenary girl I know, and there's no way she'd——'

'Sit down and be quiet!' Ross barked, his tone so fierce that she obeyed. 'I handle a trust fund for Kevin's family and he came to me today and asked for thirty thousand pounds.'

Abby was horrified by the amount. 'Maybe he had to settle a gambling debt. After all, he met Caroline at the Kitty Club, and——'

'He isn't a gambler. He went there in the first place to attend a stag party for a friend. Anyway, I know why he wanted the money. I said I wouldn't agree to release unless he told me why he wanted such a large amount.'

'You mean Caroline *asked* him for it?' Abby said incredulously.

'In a roundabout way.'

'What does that mean?'

'She used her good-for-nothing husband. He contacted Kevin and said he'd had her watched.' Ross crossed his legs and she saw the muscles flex along his thighs. Not wanting to be accused of doing the same thing as him, she quickly averted her gaze. 'He said he wouldn't contest the divorce nor ask for custody rights to his son, if Kevin made it worth his while.'

'And you believe Caroline was in cahoots with him?'

'Damn right I do!'

Abby laughed in his face. 'If you'd taken up my offer to meet her, you'd know how wrong you are. A girl who nearly starved to death rather than ask her family for help isn't likely to go to a husband she despises to extort money from a man she loves!'

'Do you honestly believe her husband did it off his own bat?' Ross shook his head. 'No, the whole thing was a shake-down.'

'You're crazy! Caroline wouldn't go back to Jeffrey if he had a million pounds, let alone thirty thousand.'

'I'm not saying she'd go back to him. Merely that they'd split the money. You know the old adage about a bird in the hand... And she's by no means sure Kevin's feelings for her will last. This way, she'd be sure of getting *something*.'

Rage rendered Abby speechless, and she banged her glass down so hard on the table next to her that liquid spattered across the polished wood surface.

'Why do you always assume the worst of people?' she stormed when she was finally able to talk. 'She loves Kevin and——'

'It's easy to love a rich young man,' Ross cut in.

'And easy to love a rich young woman. How would you feel if I accused *you* of wanting to marry Elize for her money, instead of for love?'

Black eyebrows rose superciliously. 'I happen to have enough of my own. Anyway we're not discussing me.' His jaw thrust forward. 'I suggest you pass my warning to your cousin.'

'Like hell I will! Do your own dirty work.'

Ross sighed and rose. 'I wish you'd see it from my point of view, for a change,' he said with quiet force. 'You accuse me of being biased, but I can say the same of you. You're fond of Caroline and are blind to her faults.'

'I'm not a fool. No one's perfect, but I believe totally in her honesty.'

'Then there's nothing more to be said. I'm sorry to have kept you from your dinner,' he said politely. 'I hope it won't be spoiled.'

'If it is, I'll ask Coopers' for a refund! I'm trying out your ready-prepared meals to see how they compare with those of your rivals.'

He managed a thin smile. 'How are we doing so far?'

'Very well.' Refusing to enter into further conversation with him, she went into the hall.

'Before I leave, I want to thank you for the excellent publicity you're getting us,' he said. 'I wouldn't want you to think I'm not aware of it.'

'I'm sure you don't miss anything that goes on in your business, Ross. That's one reason for its success.'

He acknowledged the compliment with a brief nod, and moved to the door. As he did, the entry-phone buzzed, and he waited while she answered it.

To her surprise it was Caroline, and Abby pressed the release catch to open the door downstairs.

'It looks as if you're going to meet my cousin whether you want to or not,' she told Ross. 'Unless you care to leave via the fire escape?'

'That's for burglars and married women's lovers,' he answered. 'And since I'm neither——' The bell rang and he stood back as Caroline stepped into the hall.

In a dark blue tracksuit that had seen better days, and with no make-up, she looked the hard-working, tired young mother she was. Recognising Ross from Abby's description of him, painful colour flooded her face.

'I—er—I'm sorry to barge in on you but I know you wanted this report urgently, and I've just finished it.'

'You were at the office till now?' Abby was dismayed.

'It's OK, Mrs Wilson loves giving Charlie his bath.'

'It could still have waited till tomorrow.'

Caroline shrugged and handed over a bulky manila envelope, then backed away.

'Don't go,' Abby said. 'I want to introduce you to Mr Hunt.'

Keeping her voice and face expressionless, she did so. Her cousin's colour deepened again as Ross subjected her to an intense appraisal, and the hand she held out to him was visibly shaking as he engulfed it in his.

'May I give you a lift home?' he asked unexpectedly.

'Not unless you live in south London.' She smiled at his obvious dismay. 'Not to worry; I'm used to buses.'

'Stay and have something to eat first. I want to go over the report with you, anyway,' Abby intervened before Ross could recover himself and repeat his offer. Not that he was doing it out of politeness. The cunning swine obviously wanted to see if he could trap her cousin into admitting she was in league with Jeffrey.

'I'll be off, then,' he said, the set of his mouth showing he knew exactly why Abby had proffered the invitation.

As the door closed behind him she expelled a sigh of relief, acknowledging how vulnerable he made her feel. Vulnerable and furious. It was an uncomfortable mix of emotions.

'I really am sorry for barging in the way I did,' Caroline apologised. 'I nearly had a fit when I saw who was here. I didn't know the big boss was on visiting terms.'

'He isn't.'

'Who was it then—his *doppelgänger*?'

Abby shuddered. 'How awful to think he might have a double. One of him is bad enough!'

'To work for, perhaps. But socially, I'd say he was every girl's idea of Prince Charming.'

'With Elize as his princess, so quit with the matchmaking.' Abby forced a smile. 'Let me put another casserole in the microwave, then we can talk as we eat.'

Ten minutes later they were seated opposite each other in the small kitchen, partaking of a delicious precooked meal, washed down with the equally delicious white wine. Only then did Abby tell her cousin why Ross had come to see her, deciding it was better for her to hear of his accusation from someone who loved her, than from Kevin, who might also harbour doubts as to her innocence.

'I can understand Ross saying what he did,' Caroline said surprisingly. 'After all, he doesn't know me, and——'

'He refused to meet you!'

'Because he's obstinate. Most men are. The more you push, the more they'll resist.'

'Where did *you* learn to be so clever?'

'I went to a tough school called "marriage to Jeffrey".'

Abby sighed. 'What are you going to do about him?'

'Change to a really nasty lawyer and tell him to pull out all the stops. Jeffrey is a bully, and when he's threatened, he'll collapse. Don't look so worried; things will work out. I feel it in my bones.'

'I'm glad one of us is optimistic.' Abby hesitated, then said, 'When Kevin's given it more thought, he might also believe the same as Ross.'

Caroline absorbed this in silence, then shook her head. 'I spoke to him tonight and he was as loving as always. If he had any doubts he'd have changed his mind about my moving.'

'Moving?'

'Yes. He's asked me to move in with him. He has his own house in St John's Wood.'

'Do you consider that wise?' Abby asked gently. 'You haven't known each other long.'

'Long enough to realise we love each other. I know you think I'm rushing things, but living with someone is the best way of getting to know them.'

'Who suggested it?'

'He did, of course. Be happy for me, darling. I know I'm doing the right thing.'

'Of course I'm happy for you. Kevin seems a sweetie.'

'He is. And Charlie adores him. I've found a lovely nursery school for him, and Kevin's daily is happy to collect him and look after him each day till I get back.'

Abby was glad her cousin's life was working out so well, yet felt she had to sound a warning. 'Don't discount Ross's influence over Kevin. They're very close.'

'I know. But if Kevin doesn't trust me, the sooner I find out the better.'

It was an hour later when Caroline left, and Abby insisted she take a cab and charge it to the company.

'You came here to deliver a report,' she said, stifling her cousin's protest at the expense, 'and there's no reason why you should be inconvenienced by it.'

'You're so good to me,' Caroline gulped, hugging Abby close. 'I wish *you'd* find someone to love. What fun if I timed my second baby to arrive with your first!'

'Don't jump the gun. I haven't even met Mr Right.'

If she said it often enough she might come to believe it, Abby thought as she turned off the hall light and finally collapsed on the sofa. So much for her restful evening! She was as exhausted as if she had run a four-minute mile.

Breathing slowly and deeply she tried to free her mind of thought, but to no avail. Ross persisted in filling it.

How would he react when he discovered Caroline had moved in with Kevin? If he tried to exert any influence over him and caused their break-up...

Her breathing quickened and she sat up straight, trying to see the situation through his eyes—as he had asked her to—and wishing again her cousin had not acted so precipitately. Without doubt he would see it as a further sign of Kevin's entrapment, and while Abby knew the girl was motivated by love, Ross was unlikely to be so generous in his assessment.

CHAPTER ELEVEN

ABBY was leaving her apartment block the following morning when she almost collided with a young man carrying an enormous bouquet of long-stemmed tea roses.

'You Miss Stewart?' he enquired.

'You're in luck!'

'So are you!' he grinned, thrusting the bouquet into her arms.

There were at least ten dozen blooms, their colours ranging from yellow to deepest peachy red. 'How gorgeous!' she exclaimed, and thought only Enrico could have sent such a lavish gift.

Returning to her apartment, she placed the flowers in the sink, tore open the envelope attached to the wrapping, and took out a plain white card with a single line of heavy black writing.

'Forgive me—Ross.'

Her heart seemed to turn over in her breast as she leaned against the wall. The brief apology was typical of the man, and was exactly what she would have expected had she been expecting an apology from him. It was also capable of two interpretations and she wondered which one he meant. Was he apologising for his accusations about Caroline, or his behaviour towards *her*? It was an answer she would know in the fullness of time.

Delving into her china cupboard, she brought out all the vases she had, but though she filled them to capacity, there were so many blooms left over that she had to place them in a sink full of water until she returned later with some containers from the office.

By the time she had placed the vases around her apartment, it resembled a florist's and had the heady fragrance of a perfume shop. Ross certainly wasn't a man for half-measures! Smiling, she reached for the telephone, and simultaneously it rang.

'I was just going to call you,' she said as she heard his voice at the other end. 'The flowers are gorgeous. Thank you very much.'

'How about the message?' His voice was deep and incisive. 'Do you?'

'How could I not?' she said softly. 'Though I'm not sure what you're apologising *for*.'

'Don't rub it in,' he said wryly. 'I've too many things to apologise for where you're concerned.'

'Don't fret yourself, Ross. Your flowers have put you in credit!'

'I chose them because they reminded me of you.'

'Tall, thin, and thorny?'

'Tall, slender, and golden.'

So he could be charming and winning when he chose, she thought with amusement.

'I appreciate the thought,' she said aloud.

'Then transfer thought into action and spend the day with me.'

'The day? You mean *now*?'

'Why not? I'll cancel my appointments if you'll do the same.'

It was terribly tempting but she resisted it. 'I have meetings throughout the day.'

'Say you have to spend it with a very demanding client. You won't even be lying!'

She smiled at the receiver, pleased he could not see it. 'Couldn't we have dinner together instead?' she suggested.

'We'll do that as *well*,' he stated. 'How soon can you be ready?'

Still she hesitated. What sort of relationship did he have with Elize that he could suggest spending the day with another woman? Or did he regard himself as fancy-free until he married? Of course there was a second possibility: that he wasn't as committed to Elize as she made out. The thought was so gratifying that she was unwilling to dwell on it.

'Give me an hour to call my clients,' she said, amazed to find herself agreeing, 'and tell me where we're going, so I'll know what to wear.'

'Wrap up warmly and bring some sensible shoes along,' he said, before ringing off.

Intrigued and excited, Abby rearranged her appointments, then changed into a hand-cabled cream cashmere tunic and matching ski pants. The man wasn't yet born who could resist a young woman wrapped in softest cashmere!

'Stunning,' Ross pronounced when he saw her. 'And mighty expensive too, if I'm any judge.'

'Too expensive for *my* pocket,' she admitted frankly. 'It was a thank-you gift from the makers for the work I did for them.'

'You've certainly come down-market with Coopers',' he teased. 'If I'm as pleased with you as they obviously were, the most you can expect from us is a case of pre-cooked dinners!'

She was still chuckling at this as they went downstairs. Ross was driving a bright red Morgan today, and when she commented on it he gave a wry grin.

'A hangover from my youth,' he explained as she fastened her safety belt. 'I hope you don't mind driving with the hood down?'

'Not as long as you promise to keep the heater going full blast!'

He set the car in motion, content not to talk while he manoeuvred through the mid-week traffic. Abby was content to be silent, for as usual she found his proximity disturbing.

He was holding the wheel lightly, his long fingers curling over the rim, one elbow resting on the side of the door. His hair was ruffled by the breeze, giving him a devil-may-care air emphasised by his casual clothes: knitted jacket in heather-tone marl with conker-brown buttons, a fine wool shirt in a toning colour, and brown trousers.

As though sensing her scrutiny, he slanted her a glance from glinting grey eyes. Her heart thumped in her breast. How easily he could arouse her.

'Am I now allowed to know where we're going?'

'The river,' he told her, and laughed at her surprise. 'I know it's winter, but it's a beautiful day, and I thought we'd take out my boat and have a picnic lunch.'

'We'll have to buy some food.'

'It's all taken care of. Just relax and enjoy yourself.'

They reached the Chiswick flyover and he pressed his foot hard on the accelerator. The concrete of Heathrow Airport whizzed by, and the tedious uniformity of the motorway was soon overtaken by the fields and hedgerows of the narrower country roads leading to Marlow, where his boat was moored.

It was a thirty-foot, six-berth cabin cruiser, paintwork shining white, brass polished to gleaming brilliance, and the name *Perfection* painted in bold black lettering on the prow.

'Like the Morgan, I don't make as much use of it as I should,' he informed her as he carried the picnic hamper, prepared by his cook, into the small, perfectly equipped galley. 'But nothing relaxes me more than chugging up and down the river.'

'Have you ever ventured further afield?' she asked.

'Not in this. But I've spent a few holidays with friends cruising the Mediterranean in a hired boat with crew. One day I'll turn this in and get something seaworthy.'

The thought of Elize sharing it with him brought a pang of jealousy, reminding her not to read too much into this day.

'One of my dreams is to own a boat,' she admitted.

'What stops you?'

'The expense.'

'Surely your parents——'

'I keep *myself*.'

'Miss Independent, eh?' he teased. 'So how about doing something equally praiseworthy and making us some coffee while I cast off?'

It was a tired and happy Abby who returned to Highgate at eleven-thirty that night. Ross had been an attentive, amusing companion, as well as a perfect gentleman, and the hours had flown by.

They had eaten lunch in the main cabin, and Abby had been unstinting in her praise of the smoked salmon, lobster salad packed in ice, home-made bread and mayonnaise, and lavish dessert of chocolate mousse and succulent raspberries. With it, Ross served Roederer champagne, though he only drank two glasses himself.

'I hope you don't expect me to finish the rest of the bottle?' she smiled.

'I certainly do!' He gave a wolfish grin. 'How else can I have my evil way with you?'

'You mean you like your women drunk and incapable?'

'Not if there's another way!' The glitter in his eyes
intensified as he half bent towards her. 'Is there?'

'No,' she said firmly.

'In that case, I'll order another bottle with dinner!'

'You mean you were serious about spending the
evening with me as well?'

'I'd be serious about spending the night with you too.'

She made herself laugh, as if it were a joke, though
the intentness of his expression told her it wasn't.

'*I'll* make the coffee this time,' he said, and she knew
his change of subject was deliberate. Clever Ross. Having
made his hopes clear, he was also making it clear he
wasn't going to put any pressure on her. Not that pressure
was needed. The mere proximity of him was like flame
to her tinder!

Lunch over, they idly cruised the river, lazing away
the afternoon and early evening in idle talk and con-
tented silences before returning to their mooring berth.

They dined at an elegant inn near Bray, seated at a
window table overlooking the darkening water. Neither
of them was hungry and they ordered a light meal of
poached trout, followed by a Grand Marnier soufflé.
Only when they were at the coffee stage did Ross refer
to Caroline.

'As soon as I met her I realised I'd misjudged her,'
he confessed. 'It was a happy coincidence her turning
up at your place last night. It gave me the chance to see
why Kevin has fallen for her. Apart from being very
pretty, there's a touching vulnerability about her.'

'Kevin said the same,' Abby murmured casually, as if
Ross were saying exactly what she had expected.

'I still feel they should take things slowly,' he went
on. 'She's had one unhappy experience, and she might
well fall for him on the rebound.'

'I doubt it. She's been separated from her husband
for nearly a year.'

'That's still early days.'

Abby diplomatically said nothing, and Ross continued speaking.

'I gather Kevin offered to help her financially but she refused, which made his family breathe easier, and my advice, if you see fit to pass it on, is for her to remain independent of him in every way till her divorce comes through.'

'What do you mean by "every way"?' Abby asked with a sinking heart.

'That she doesn't move in with him before their relationship has had a chance to develop. Otherwise they'd really think she was trying to get her hooks into him.'

'Who's the "they" you keep referring to?' Abby couldn't refrain from asking, even though she knew damn well who one of them was.

'Elize and her mother,' Ross said calmly. 'They are a wealthy family and——'

'They can't believe anyone could love Kevin for himself,' Abby finished, annoyance getting the better of discretion. 'I can understand someone thinking that of Elize, who acts like a velvet slipper but is tough as old boots, but Kevin would be fanciable even if he didn't have a penny!'

'I agree,' Ross said smoothly. 'But your cousin's already had one failed marriage, and his mother and sister feel neither of them should rush into anything.'

Abby swallowed a retort, determined not to spoil this lovely day by saying anything to provoke an argument; their new-found harmony was too tenuous to risk. As she had feared, Kevin had not been completely truthful with his family. Yet with Caroline moving into his home soon, how long did he hope to keep her presence there a secret? And why, at his age, should he need to? She nibbled at her lip. It looked as if there was a weakness in his character that made him want to please everyone.

But this was not always possible, for there came a time in everyone's life when choices had to be made, and he should be man enough to make his family realise there were certain things he had to decide for himself.

'A penny for them,' Ross said.

'What?'

'Your thoughts.'

'Oh, a penny's far too low! Try half a million!'

'You must be thinking of me! Nothing else could be worth that price!'

She laughed, happy the mood had changed, and it remained light-hearted as, the bill paid, they returned to the car and headed for London.

There was little traffic and Ross drove fast. Abby sat low in her seat, glad of the thick rug he had wrapped around her, and revelling in the feeling of closeness engendered by their being cocooned in this low-slung, ancient car. Only as they approached the outskirts of the city were they stopped by a traffic light, and he turned to look at her, a smile tilting his mouth as he stretched out a hand and smoothed her tangled red-gold locks.

'You look even more beautiful when you're windblown,' he said softly.

'Then I'm glad you drove with your window down!'

'Lord! So I did. You should have asked me to close it.'

'And spoilt your fun? You loved feeling you were fighting the elements!'

He laughed. 'You're right. I did!'

Nevertheless he wound up the window as he spoke, and as he turned back to her their eyes met, hers amused, his tender, with something deeper flickering in them.

Abby felt suspended; as if she were poised on a skislope waiting for the downward run. She lowered her lids and stared at her hands, pale and ringless on her lap. If only Ross would be the man to put one there!

Suddenly she knew she was in love with him, and that above all else she wanted to share his life. Yet it was madness! Before today, nearly all their conversations had ended in argument or barely concealed hostility. Even more to the point was the presence of Elize, who was an integral part of his life and intended to keep it that way.

But how did Ross feel? It was not a question she dared ask outright, though somehow or other she had to discover the answer. Until she did, she had to put her love for him in limbo.

CHAPTER TWELVE

THE light drizzle turned into a downpour as they approached London, increasing to a torrent as they drove through Regent's Park, and it was then that the rain began leaking through the soft top of the car directly on to Ross.

He swore beneath his breath. 'The garage said they'd fixed it. I'll give them hell tomorrow.'

'That won't help you tonight! You'll be drenched by the time you get home.'

He dabbed at his wet face with his handkerchief but it was completely ineffectual, and when he drew up outside her apartment he was soaked to the skin and shivering.

'Leave your car here tonight and get your garage to collect it in the morning,' Abby suggested. 'If you come upstairs I'll call a cab for you, and while you're waiting I'll dry your things.' She gave him a mischievous grin. 'If I didn't know a dry day had been forecast, I'd have suspected this was a put-up job!'

His chuckle was cut off by a sneeze, and as soon as they entered her apartment she showed him where the bathroom was and handed him a large towel.

He accepted it and sneezed again. 'Any chance of a hot drink before you call a cab? I'm cold as hell.'

'Hell's hot, but I get your meaning!'

She was pouring instant coffee into two cups when he came into the kitchen, the towel draped toga-like around him. His chest was bare save for the thick hair scrolling upon the centre, and she tensed nervously at sight of

125

long muscular legs, only relaxing as she caught sight of
white briefs covering narrow hips.

'Sorry for undressing like this,' he apologised, 'but
my trousers were dripping wet.' He indicated the bundle
of clothes he was holding. 'If you'll show me where your
drier is...'

She did, taking them from him as he went to squash
them into the machine. 'If you don't fold your things
properly, they'll come out looking as if you've had them
pleated!'

'I don't care as long as they're dry. Giorgio will soon
get them into shape.'

'Is he your valet as well as your butler?' she asked,
placing the clothes in the drier and turning it on.

'He and his wife are my treasures,' Ross answered.
'One reason I've resisted marriage is that my home is
run so perfectly I don't want a wife coming along and
spoiling it!'

Not sure if he was joking, Abby said nothing, going
ahead of him into the living-room and placing his coffee
on a little table in front of an armchair, before settling
herself on the sofa.

If he noticed the way she engineered the seating ar-
rangements, he gave no sign of it, dropping into the chair
and gratefully sipping the hot drink.

'Don't I make you feel overdressed?' he teased.

'I think the correct line is, "wouldn't you like to slip
into something more comfortable?"'

'Well, wouldn't you?' In one lithe movement he left
his chair and joined her on the sofa. 'I'd be happy to
assist. It's an art I've practised to perfection!'

'I bet you have. But the answer's no.'

'Your eyes say something different.'

'Try reading my palm!'

'And I love your sense of humour.' His voice
deepened. 'We'd make lovely music together.'

'I was under the impression you had an orchestra going with Elize.'

There, it was out, and Abby wouldn't have had it unsaid. Indeed she wished she had said it at the beginning of the day, instead of allowing herself to live in a fool's paradise. A man ready to cheat on one woman would have no hesitation in cheating on another, and she needed to be the 'other' like she needed a hole in her head!

'If I were serious about Elize I wouldn't be here with you,' Ross said flatly. 'I've known her most of my life and we're good friends. Nothing more.'

'*Very* good friends from what she said.'

Only then did Ross show signs of discomfort. 'I've never given her any reason to think other than what I've just told you. If she does, it's wishful thinking. Women tend to indulge in it.'

Abby could understand why they did—where he was concerned. After all, she had done a fair amount of it over him herself.

'But you do date Elize,' she persisted.

'I date many girls. But I haven't wanted any of them since I met you.'

'I bet you're a marvellous fisherman, Ross.'

'Come again?'

'You cast a wonderful line!'

His mouth quirked in a smile and she put her thumb to it and traced the edge of his upper lip. 'I'm sorry, Ross, but I don't go in for one-night stands. It's a decision I made years ago and I haven't regretted it.'

'A one-night stand wasn't what I had in mind.' His eyes, dark grey with intensity, bore into hers. 'You bowled me over the moment I saw you at the Kitty Club. I despised myself for it but I couldn't stop thinking of you. If you hadn't waltzed into my life again, I'd have gone back there to see you.'

'You're kidding!'

'No,' he groaned, sliding nearer and pulling her close. 'I'm crazy for you. You're the sexiest, most adorable, intelligent, infuriating and exasperating creature I know, and I want to——'

What he wanted was never said, for action replaced words and his mouth came down hard and hot on hers. His bare skin was warm, his shoulders broad, and as he pushed her back upon the sofa she felt the hardness of his body pressing down the length of her, and the steel strength of his thighs heavy on hers.

Expecting his passion to intensify, she was surprised when the pressure of his mouth softened and he made no effort to force her lips apart, content to partially rest upon her, most of his weight taken by the cushions as his hand gently caressed the curve of her cheek.

'I've never felt like this for a woman,' he murmured. 'Sometimes you've made me so furious I could have wrung your neck, but at other times I've wanted to hold you—as I'm doing now—and feel your body curving into mine.'

'You probably thought it was the best way of shutting me up!'

His soft laugh held tenderness. 'You could be right. The way you answer back turns me on, which is why I've had more cold showers these past weeks than at any other time in my life!'

'Maybe you should have one now,' Abby said shakily.

'Worried I'll lose control?' Thumb beneath her chin, he turned her face to his. 'I won't force you to do anything you don't want to do, sweetheart, though I have to confess this is the first time I've lain on a sofa with a girl and just necked with her!'

'There's a first time for everything.'

'And you're the first girl I'm happy to do it with.'

Joy coursed through her and she turned her body fully towards him. He wrapped his arms round her and she experienced a deep sense of homecoming, as if she had known this man for years rather than a matter of months.

His lips found hers again, and this time hers parted of their own volition. For a split second he hesitated, then his tongue drove into her, its heat and sweetness arousing her to a passion that made her cling to him, coherent thought gone, swept away by a need as deep as his to hold and touch. As her fingers lightly skimmed across his skin, his muscles tensed, and against her side she felt the burgeoning swell of his arousal.

'Darling,' he said thickly, and twined his arms around her as if trying to fuse their bodies into one.

For what seemed eternity they clung to each other, his darting tongue a flame arousing her to a burning need that craved fulfilment. She moaned deep in her throat and, taking it as acquiescence, he effortlessly swung her up into his arms, stepped over the white towel that fell away from his body, and carried her across the living-room to the bedroom.

Gently placing her on the bed, he lay down beside her and with practised ease undressed her, all the while caressing her with his tongue; sucking the tips of her hard, rosy nipples until she writhed in a shuddering agony of desire, licking the soft swell of her belly, then moving lower to the pulsating mound between her legs.

'Is this what you like, darling?' he whispered. 'Or is it this?' His hand found the moist, tumescent peak, and the tips of his fingers rubbed slowly and deliberately over it. 'Or this?' he questioned, as the invasion became penetratingly intimate.

She moved frantically beneath him, and responding to the powerful urgency of her passion, he guided her hand to the pulsating thickness between his legs.

'Touch me,' he groaned. 'Hold me.'

The exquisite feel of him, silky hard in her palms, turned her bones to liquid and brought her nerve-ends quiveringly alive. This was a depth of passion she had never known, and she delighted in pleasuring him as he was pleasuring her. He swelled and grew harder, rubbing his organ on the soft skin of her inner thigh until she caught it close with both hands and, spreading her legs apart, guided him into her.

He filled her with his bulk and she wrapped her slender legs around his muscular thighs and absorbed him fully into her. Linking his hands with hers on the pillows above, he lightly covered her lips with his. But there was no urgency in him, no attempt to hurry. This first union was a moment to be savoured and enjoyed to the utmost.

Slowly his hips began to undulate, making each thrust long and deep, and Abby gloried in her body's respon- siveness as she matched him stroke for stroke. In and out, up and down, the pace increased fiercely, urgently, dominantly, and she raked her nails across his back and buttocks, and cried his name, knowing this was what she had been waiting for; what she had wanted all her adult life. This man, who felt so right inside her, who made her ache for him, who transported her to undreamt ecstasy.

The first contraction of pleasure surged through her like an electric current, and as wave upon wave con- vulsed her, Ross too lost control, pounding her, filling her, flooding her with his life force as he reached a vi- olent, shuddering climax.

Tears spurted from her eyes and she gasped and cried his name, burying her face into his sweat-streaked hair as he collapsed on her and rested his head upon her breast.

'I love you,' she whispered, and waited for him to echo it, but all she heard was the soft sigh of his breath as his body grew lax with sleep. Darling Ross, she thought, then joined him in sleep.

Abby awoke to find herself alone in bed, and the quietness told her Ross had gone. Though disappointed he hadn't stayed, she knew why. He had a seven-thirty breakfast meeting in the City, and had they woken up together he might not have made it in time! Lazily she stretched, a sensuous smile curving her lips as she saw the indent of his head on the pillow beside her, and recalled their lovemaking. Incredibly he had taken her twice more in the night, devouring her with a bold hunger she had easily matched.

Had her love for him made her respond with such abandonment? Or was it because he was a passionate and considerate lover, always alert to her needs, and satisfying them before considering his own fulfilment?

Whatever, she had no regrets. How could she when she was so sublimely happy and wonderfully alive? The alarm buzzed, reminding her this was a working day for her too, and leaving the warmth of the duvet, she headed for the bathroom.

Soaping herself under the shower she was pulsatingly alive to her body, aware of it in a way she hadn't been before. Her breasts were tender to the touch, the nipples still tingling from Ross's suckling, while faint bruises on her waist were evidence of his passionate hold as he had penetrated deeper and deeper into her. She trembled at the memory and the soap slipped from her grasp. Leaving it foaming in the water, she turned off the shower and reached for her towelling robe, wrapping it round her as she padded into the kitchen to make some coffee.

As she sipped it, she visualised Ross sitting opposite her, and the breakfast she would make him. It wouldn't compare to the sumptuous one prepared by Giorgio's wife and served with such panache by Giorgio himself, although the butler couldn't offer all the things *she* could!

Smiling in anticipation of the weekend, when Ross was
sure to stay with her, she went into her room to dress.

An appointment with a client took up the entire morning,
and arriving at her office after lunch, she read through
her mail and spent half the afternoon dictating letters
to her secretary. The girl had no sooner left to transcribe
them than Caroline came in, brimming with curiosity to
know if Abby had enjoyed her day with Ross.

'It was very nice. We spent it on his boat on the
Thames. We had a picnic lunch, cruised around, and
then had dinner near Marlow.'

'I take it you no longer dislike him?'

Abby gave what she hoped was a nonchalant shrug,
but annoyingly felt her cheeks grow warm. 'I certainly
got to know him better,' she mumbled.

'How much better?'

'Hey, the Spanish Inquisition's over! What's with all
the questions?'

'I'm intrigued to know why you're blushing.' Caroline,
who had blossomed into her earlier, bubbly self since
Kevin had come on the scene, was not going to be put
off. 'I've a feeling you more than like him. That's why
you've always been sarcastic with him—as a defence
mechanism.'

'Yes, Dr Freud.'

Caroline grinned, then ceased her bantering. 'I don't
mean to be nosy, but I don't want you getting hurt.'

'Why should I?'

'Because he's handsome, brilliant, and rich, and has
the self-confidence that goes with it. He's also in his
mid-thirties and still single, which says something else
about him.'

'That he's wary.'

'Or likes playing the field. Did he—did he make a
pass at you?'

Suddenly Abby was tired of hedging. Her cousin was the nearest she had to a sister, and it would be good to be totally honest with someone.

'Yes, he did, if you must know, and I didn't resist.' Pink cheeks grew pinker, making further explanation unnecessary.

'Oh, Abby! Knowing you, that means you've fallen for him.' Caroline frowned. 'Where does Elize fit into the picture? I thought you said the two of them were buddy-buddy.'

'They are, but only because their families have known each other forever.'

There was a knock on the door, and her secretary came in with a slim package wrapped in Asprey's distinctive paper. 'A messenger just brought this for you,' she said.

Puzzled, Abby opened it and saw a small leather jewellery box. Lifting the lid, she stared at the gold brooch nestling on the black velvet lining. It was in the shape of a leaping cat, its front paws holding a diamond-studded ball, its eyes gleaming emeralds.

'Wow!' Caroline exclaimed.

Speechless, Abby read the unsigned note.

'Until I met *you* I was a doggy man.'

'I'm sure he doesn't send such expensive gifts to every woman he goes to bed with,' Caroline commented. 'Maybe he *is* serious about you.'

Trying not to look like the cat that had swallowed the canary, Abby reached for the telephone, and Caroline, guessing who she was calling, gave her a wave and went out.

To Abby's dismay, she learned Ross was visiting all his Midland stores and wouldn't be back until late Friday. 'But he'll be calling me later today,' his secretary concluded, 'and if you want to leave a message...'

Surprised he hadn't mentioned he was going out of town, she asked if he could call her at home after work.

At five o'clock she left to attend the press conference she had arranged at the Dorchester for the cosmetic company she was promoting. There was a far greater turn-out of journalists than she had anticipated, and her grateful client insisted she have dinner with him and two of his senior executives in the Grill Room afterwards.

It was nearly midnight when she returned home, and she immediately switched on her answer-phone in the hope that one of the flashing messages was from Ross. She was not disappointed.

'I intended telling you last night I'd be away for a few days, but I was otherwise diverted,' his disembodied voice informed her, 'and I didn't want to wake you before I left in case I was diverted again!' In spite of the distortion of the tape, a husky tone was clearly discernible. 'I hope you liked the present. I'll be in touch as soon as I return.'

For the rest of the week Abby immersed herself in the cookery series. Enrico had done a dummy run in the studio and had been so fantastic that she foresaw him giving up his position at Coopers' to become a full-time TV cook.

On Friday afternoon she was busily vetting some new publicity hand-outs when Elize walked in on her, elegant as always in the beautifully tailored suits she seemed to favour for her 'office wear'.

'Sorry to barge in without warning,' she apologised. 'But I was passing close by and thought it a good opportunity to ask you about the television interview I'm doing next Monday. I couldn't discuss it with you before because I was out of town with Ross.' She settled into a chair. 'I'm not sure what image you'd like me to project.'

'A natural one,' Abby said promptly. 'The camera doesn't lie, and if you put on an act, it can spot it. Just be yourself.'

'Won't I seem too sophisticated?'

Abby's eyes moved from the glossy brown bob that swung provocatively forward on to the girl's cheeks, to the small but full red mouth, and petite but curvaceous body. Knowing Ross saw the girl simply as a friend enabled her to view Elize with greater magnanimity.

'Most of the women who shop at Coopers' would give their eye teeth to look like you,' she said. 'And knowing you're the fashion buyer will make them believe they can achieve it if they buy the clothes *you've* chosen.'

'What a sweet thing to say. It means I can wear the dress Ross bought for me yesterday.'

Abby was instantly on full alert, positive this visit had nothing to do with the forthcoming interview, but everything to do with Ross. Did Elize know he had made love to her?

'It's red chiffon,' the girl went on, 'and very frilly and feminine. Hardly the sort of thing I'd have chosen myself, but he saw it in a boutique in Birmingham and insisted I try it on.'

'If Ross's clothes are anything to go by,' Abby managed to say, 'he should have excellent taste.'

'He has. But I prefer to surprise him with what I wear. I think it's important for a woman to retain her mystery with a man, don't you?'

'Oh, yes.' Raging inside but outwardly cool, Abby leaned back in her chair, her tone casual. 'I hadn't realised you'd gone to the Midlands with him. How is turnover?'

'Eight per cent up on last month. All the stores are benefiting from the promotions you're doing, and Ross is really pleased.' She flashed a smile. 'Not that our trip

was all work. We stayed over in Stratford last night to
see the new production of *Richard III*.'

Jealousy seared Abby like a red-hot poker, and the
pen she had been toying with shook in her hand. Aware
of Elize watching her, she deliberately held out her hand.

'I worked through my lunch-hour,' she lied, 'and I get
shaky if I don't eat. Care to join me for a sandwich?'
She'd choke on the food if Elize said yes, and breathed
a sigh of relief when the offer was refused.

'I have to be going. I'm having dinner with Ross, and
I want to have a leisurely bath first.'

Abby's mind was racing. Until today, the girl, though
dropping hints about her closeness to Ross, had never
actually put it into words, and it was strange she should
be doing so now.

'I've surprised you, haven't I?' Elize stated. 'I know
I've always maintained we were just friends, but the truth
is, Ross wanted me to marry him years ago but I wanted
to prove myself first. And then, when I had, he wouldn't
marry *me*.'

'Why not?' Abby marvelled that she managed to speak
when her entire body had gone numb.

'Because he insisted I stop working for the company—
said it smacked of nepotism for the chairman's wife to
do so. Nor would he let me accept a job with anyone
else. Said I was too good to go to a rival!'

'He's right.' Abby swung her chair casually from side
to side, proud of herself for appearing unconcerned. 'So
who's going to win?'

'We both are. I've proved my worth by being ap-
pointed head fashion buyer, but come the end of the
year, I'll settle for marriage. By then all Coopers' winter
clothes will be in, and I'll have placed my orders for next
spring and summer, so what better time to retire?'

'What better. But won't you regret giving up your
career?'

'Yes, but the compensations outweigh it!' Elize opened
the door and, half way out, flung her grin. 'When *you*
fall in love, Abby, you'll know what I mean.'

Alone in her office, Abby refused to give in to the
tears burning her eyes, aware that if she did she might
not stop crying for hours. And Ross wasn't worth it.
Not for a second! She was an idiot to have believed the
line he had spun her, but her idiocy stopped right here.
Grabbing her coat, she stormed from the office.

Arriving home, she wearily ran a bath, and only in
the warm, Arpège-scented water did she relax and calmly
review what she had learned this afternoon.

How long had Ross thought he could continue seeing
her without Elize discovering it? Or was he so adept at
deception that he had perfected two-timing his girlfriends to a fine art? The thought that she was probably
one of many such interludes filled her with abhorrence,
the more so as she recalled his lovemaking and her response to it. Thank goodness he had no idea she was in
love with him. Given that she was obliged to go on seeing
him for business reasons, it would have made her position even more unendurable.

The ringing of the telephone brought her out of her
unhappy reverie, and fearing it was Ross, she didn't
answer it. She had not yet decided how to handle the
situation, and wanted to mull things over before speaking
to him.

Playing back the tape, she found her guess had been
correct, for she heard his deep voice explaining he had
a business dinner and would call next day. Business
dinner indeed!

She paced the floor, too tense to read or watch television and, when she finally went to bed, too tense to
sleep. Wide awake, she relived her day with him: the
teasing, the joking, the laughter; the pleasure in discovering how similar their tastes were, even in food and

wine. It had been a day to remember, and a night of joy she would never forget.

Morning dawned, and heavy-eyed she sifted through her mail. It consisted of circulars and a couple of bills, but there was also an invitation to a party from an old friend she had not seen for months, and she quickly made up her mind to accept it. Having relegated Ross to the past tense on a personal level, she had no intention of staying home brooding. Off with the old and on with the new was her motto.

Yet realistically she knew she was clutching at straws. She had only known Ross for a short time, yet so swiftly and deeply had he penetrated her heart that it would take forever to forget him.

CHAPTER THIRTEEN

NEXT day Abby left her apartment at noon, having promised to help Caroline move into Kevin's home in the afternoon.

Expecting Ross to call first thing in the morning, she had been disconcerted when he didn't, and wondered if he had found out that Elize had seen her yesterday and told her the truth of their relationship. If so, he was unlikely to call her again! Yet she still had to see him on a business basis, and found the prospect so daunting that she seriously debated asking her father to let someone else in their office handle the account.

But thoughts of Ross vanished when, reaching the dilapidated house where her cousin lived, the landlady told her Caroline had been knocked down by a car and was in a nearby hospital.

'Is she badly hurt?' she asked in alarm.

'Cuts and bruises. You know hospitals—they don't go into detail.'

'How did it happen? She was supposed to be here, packing.'

'Not any more. Her boyfriend rang to say it was off,' the plump, grey-headed woman replied. 'Terribly upset she was. All packed and ready to go, then he did the dirty. That upset, she was. Said she had to get out of the house to think things over, and would I look after Charlie? An hour later the hospital phoned and said she'd been run over. I didn't know how to get in touch with you. All I have is the number where she works, and there was no answer from it.'

'I'll go to the hospital right away,' Abby said. 'Can you take care of Charlie till I get back?'

'Of course. He's such a good little soul, he's no trouble.'

Abby's first sight of her cousin lying in a narrow hospital bed brought a lump to her throat. Pale as the gown covering her, and bruised as a boxer who'd lost a ten-round fight, she was a travesty of the bright, beautiful girl seen yesterday at the office.

'Oh, Abby,' Caroline said weakly, tears filling her eyes. 'I'm so glad to see you.'

'Not half as glad as I am to see *you*. What did you do—hit a bus?'

'I crossed the road without looking, and stepped in front of a car.'

'You're lucky you weren't seriously injured.' Abby was aware of the triteness of her remark, but knew it was better than voicing her real fear—that Caroline had attempted to kill herself. 'The sister says you've cracked a couple of ribs and have some severe bruising, but you should be well enough to leave tomorrow.'

Caroline's eyes overflowed with tears. 'Where will I go? Kevin doesn't want me, and my room's let to someone else.'

'You can stay with my parents. They'd love to have you.' Determinedly, Abby held her sympathy in check. 'What went wrong between you and Kevin?'

'I haven't a clue. He just rang and said it was better if I didn't move in with him yet. He wouldn't say any more.'

Remembering Ross saying Kevin's family were against Caroline living with him until she was free, Abby was certain he was behind today's events. He had probably never changed his mind about her cousin, despite his fine words to the contrary. Bitterness filled her. He had known he would never get to first base with her as long as she believed he was set against Caroline, and for this reason had pretended otherwise. It had merely been a strategy to disarm and seduce her.

'Kevin's family are still worried in case you're using him as a bolt-hole,' Abby stated aloud, 'and I'm pretty sure Elize persuaded Ross to put the pressure on him.'

'But you said Ross liked me!'

'I guess it suited him to pretend.'

'I never thought Kevin was so weak. I'm a rotten picker of men.'

'I'm not too good myself. I believed Ross meant what he said about you. If I hadn't, I'd never have...'

Her voice trailed away, and Caroline agitatedly reached for her hand.

'Don't let what's occurred between Kevin and myself interfere with you and Ross.'

'How can it not? I couldn't have a future with a man who'd lie in order to get me into bed. Anyway, he's committed to Elize. They're getting married at the end of the year.'

'But——'

'It's true,' Abby cut in. 'So let's drop the subject.'

Shortly afterwards she returned to her cousin's flat to collect some toiletries and nightwear. She also called her parents to put them in the picture, and they immediately offered to collect Charlie and look after him.

'I'll bring him over to you myself,' Abby said. 'I'll take Caroline a few toiletries and come back to collect the baby. There's one other thing, Dad,' she continued reluctantly. 'Ross has never liked Caroline, and I'm sure he's behind Kevin's behaviour. I want to talk to him, but if I do, there's a chance we'll have a furious row and will lose the Coopers' account.'

'I see. Well, actually I don't. Can you give me a few more details?'

'It's rather personal. It's a question of lies and pretence. Honestly, Dad, a straightforward disagreement I could handle, but Ross was so devious...' Too choked to continue, she fell silent.

'I know the account means a lot to you, my dear, and if you're prepared to run the risk of losing it... Well, it's your choice.'

'Thanks, Dad. You're an angel.'

'Not for twenty years yet, I hope!'

Relieved to have her father's approval, Abby drove back to the hospital. It would be late afternoon before she dropped Charlie off at her parents'. Was that too late to call Ross and ask if he were free to see her? She didn't know what his plans were for the weekend— probably to get her into bed again, unless it was Elize's turn for his affections. Her blood boiled at the very thought, and was still bubbling when she walked down the hospital corridor and saw him sitting near Sister's office.

At sight of her, he rose and came striding towards her. 'Abby! I just called you again and left another message on your answer-phone.'

'What the hell are *you* doing here?' she demanded, stopping well short of his reach and ignoring what he had said.

Startled by the rudeness of her greeting, he hesitated momentarily. 'I came down with Kevin.'

'He's here too? What a nerve! It's *his* behaviour that's put Caroline in hospital.'

'That's why he's here. She was moving in with him today, as I'm sure you know.' Implicit in Ross's tone was that Abby had not seen fit to mention it to him. 'But it wasn't until he told her the arrangement had to be put off that he learned her landlady had already let the rooms she'd been occupying, so he spent the morning trying to find another place for her. When he rang to say he'd found one, he discovered she was in hospital. He was so distraught when he called me, I didn't want him driving here alone. He's with her now.'

'Sweet of him to go to so much trouble. Men who ditch girls don't usually bother.'

'He didn't ditch her.'

'Really? What would you call it? A change of heart due to family pressure?'

'The family had nothing to do with it.' Unusually fidgety, Ross put his hands into the pockets of his trousers. It hunched his shoulders and made them look broader. 'I'm sorry we couldn't meet last night, but I had a business dinner.'

With Elize in a red chiffon dress, Abby thought bitterly, but played dumb.

'Then this morning I had a breakfast meeting,' he went on, 'and by the time I called you, you'd gone out.'

He looked her full in the face, his expression strained, and she wondered if his conscience was prickling him. It damn well should, considering all the lies he had told, to say nothing of being partly responsible for her cousin's accident.

'I'm afraid I won't be able to see you for a while,' he continued into the silence. 'I'm going to be tied up with a new acquisition.'

'Anything I can publicise?' Her tone was one of sweetness and interest.

'No, no, I—er—I want to keep it under wraps. But I'll see you again as soon as things are easier.'

Had she required further proof of his involvement with Elize, she was being given it with a vengeance.

'I'd rather you didn't,' she said airily. 'I'd prefer to make the break permanent. It's not good to mix business with pleasure. It can get messy.'

'That wasn't the signal you gave me the other night.'

'That was then,' she shrugged, 'and this is now. I'm sure you see it my way too.'

'Because I said I'll be tied up for some time? I'm not giving you the brush-off, Abby. I really have——'

Her little trill of laughter cut him short. 'Don't make excuses, Ross, it isn't necessary. We had a wonderful day and it ended with a wonderful night. But it's ended.'

She went to move past him, not sure how long she could maintain her act, but he blocked her way.

'Do you blame me for Kevin's behaviour? Is that why you're saying all this?'

It was a temptation to say yes, but saving her face was a greater temptation, and she forced herself to stay calm.

'I certainly think you had something to do with it,' she answered. 'You were against Caroline from the start, and I don't believe you ever changed your opinion of her.'

'You mean I was lying the other day when I said I liked her?'

'I think you said it because you knew it would please me.'

An angry breath hissed between Ross's teeth. 'You believe I said it as a sweetener to get you into bed? Do you think I'm so low—or so desperate to get a woman?'

Abby shrugged, as if the question were no longer important, but deep down, her fury was as intense as the passion she had felt for him, though there was no joy in it, merely a burning desire to wound.

'I was a challenge to you, Ross, as you were to me. But we both won, so let's leave it at that. I'm just sorry you have so much influence over Kevin. How did you get him to change his mind yesterday? Did you threaten to fire him, or play Scrooge again with his trust fund?'

Ross stared at her without replying, his pallor and the clenching of his hands the only signs of temper. She waited for him to say he no longer wanted her company to work for him, and when he didn't, felt a momentary triumph, quickly followed by bitterness. Despite her rudeness to him, he knew he had hired one of the best public relations companies in the country, and had no intention of doing anything to jeopardise their working relationship. Clever Ross; as expedient in business as in his personal life.

With a toss of her head she swept past him and entered the amenity room where Caroline lay. Kevin was sitting by her bed, and both looked flushed and emotional. He greeted her quietly and offered her his chair—there was no other in the room—but she refused it.

'I'm not staying. I popped in to give Caroline these.' Abby placed the parcel she had brought with her in the little cabinet by the bed. 'I'm taking Charlie to my parents',' she informed her cousin, 'so unless you want him completely spoiled, you'd better get out of here fast!'

'The doctor came in while you were away and said I can leave tomorrow after lunch.'

'Great.' Abby paused, and when Kevin remained silent, added brightly: 'I'll pick you up at two. I already have your cases in my car.'

'You're such a darling. I don't know how I'd cope without you.'

'That's what families are for.' Abby glanced at Kevin with such contempt that he turned brick red.

'I'd best be pushing off,' he muttered, leaning forward to place a hasty kiss on Caroline's mouth. 'I'll be in touch.'

As the door closed behind him, Abby swung round to her cousin. 'I've heard of turning the other cheek, but how can you even bear to see him... Why didn't you throw him out?'

'I love him.'

'So you'll let him play fast and loose with you?'

'He isn't. He has problems and has to sort them out by himself.'

'He certainly has problems,' Abby snapped. 'And with big sister and Ross on his back, he won't sort them out.'

'I don't agree with you, and I'd rather we dropped the subject.'

Caroline was so pale that Abby was instantly contrite. Her cousin was a far softer character than she herself, and to expect her to act strongly was asking the impossible. The poor darling had to learn the hard way that Kevin was a weakling, controlled by others.

Promising to return early next afternoon, Abby hurried out.

There was no sign of Ross, and she sighed with relief. If only she didn't have to continue seeing him and pretend she was indifferent to him. But unless he cancelled their contract, there was no way of avoiding it. The test would come soon enough, for he was booked to appear on a popular chat show next Friday evening, and she was to accompany him to the studio.

There was no word from him the entire week, and early Friday she instructed her secretary to call him and say a studio car was collecting him at five-thirty. 'Say I'll meet him there,' she added.

Entering the TV company's hospitality room late that afternoon, Ross's eyes met hers with a directness that held no trace of embarrassment. How little their quarrel had affected him! Anger leavened her nervousness and helped her regain her composure.

'Nice to see you,' he said formally, holding out a chair.

His face was devoid of expression and she knew he was waiting for her to speak. Did he imagine she was going to act as if nothing had happened? Whatever was in his mind he had no intention of divulging it.

Digging her hands into the pockets of her jacket, she leaned back in the chair. She was unaware of the delectably feminine picture she made; her oval-shaped face rising from a swath of scarlet silk, a few tendrils of red-gold hair curling against her ears.

'Gary will be in soon to introduce himself.' Her voice was loud to her ears, and she lowered it. 'They'll be serving drinks too.'

'I've done television interviews before, Abby, I know the form.'

'Of course. I'd forgotten.'

'In fact, there was no need for you to come. I've managed without a nanny since I was a child.'

'It's part of my job to be here,' she replied, ignoring the sarcasm. 'Besides, I didn't want you thinking I was avoiding you.'

There was an awkward silence, thankfully relieved by the appearance of the host, Gary Winton, and his other guests, two famous actor brothers appearing in a film together. After introducing everyone, drinks and snacks were offered round, and Abby noticed that Ross declined any alcohol. Not for him an artificial confidence booster! In a formal charcoal pin-stripe suit and plain white shirt, he was in complete contrast to the casual appearance of his host and the movie stars. It set him apart, as did his air of command, which marked him out as a man used to power, and despite her antipathy towards him, she felt a surge of pride at the way he out-shone the two younger heart-throbs.

'I'll take you on to the set now, and familiarise you with it,' Gary announced, including Abby in the invitation.

The studio was the largest in the building, and was bustling with cameramen and technicians. A range of cameras were banked along one side, facing a contemporary set in chrome and black leather.

'You're the first one on tonight,' Gary told Ross, showing him which entrance to take when his name was called. 'I'm glad he realised all work and no play makes dull viewing,' he added in a whispered aside to Abby. 'We should get an interesting interview now.'

Puzzled by what he meant, she had no chance to ask him, for the audience was being ushered into the studio, and Gary remained to welcome them. Of Ross and the other two guests there were no sign, for they had been whisked off for last-minute adjustments to their make-up.

Abby retired to the hospitality room to watch the interview on a TV monitor. Her nervousness made nonsense of her attempt to convince herself she regarded Ross as just another client. No matter how much she despised him, she still loved him!

Ross's interview went as she had envisaged; he was confident and lucid and the dialogue flowed freely. He frequently scored points against his host, and was loudly applauded by the audience. But unexpectedly the whole tenor of the conversation changed when Gary suddenly referred to Ross's private life, and the women he had dated.

Abby was flummoxed. Gary had promised to lay off all personal questions, and she was amazed he had broken his word, for he had never done so before.

Despite being caught unawares, Ross did not lose his cool, and answered wittily and with panache. But Gary was not to be put off.

'You've escorted many beautiful women, and have a reputation for loving and leaving them,' he commented, listing some of the well-known beauties with whom Ross's name had been linked. 'Is that because you don't believe in marriage?'

'On the contrary. I believe in it implicitly. And when I do marry, it will be for life. That's why, until the right woman says yes, I'll continue loving and leaving!'

'Sounds as though you've already met her. Care to comment?'

'No.'

Gary was not to be dissuaded. 'Rumour has it you're seriously involved with someone, and that your bachelor days are numbered.' He turned towards the audience with a conspiratorial smile. 'I'd like to name the lucky girl, but I'd better leave it to the prospective bridegroom.' He faced his guest again. 'How about it, Ross?'

'I'd rather wait for the gossip columnists to announce it,' Ross replied smoothly. 'If I pre-empt them, they might stop mentioning my name in their columns—and bang goes free publicity for Coopers'!'

The audience laughed and clapped, and giving Gary no chance to return to the subject, Ross channelled the conversation to out-of-town shopping precincts and their effect on high street trade.

Abby was livid with Gary for breaking his word to her, and though anxiously waiting for Ross to return to the hospitality room, found herself wondering if someone at Coopers' had tipped off Gary about Elize. Perhaps they had seen them exchanging the sort of looks that lovers often did, even when they wanted to keep their liaison secret.

The very thought of their intimacy was like a fire inside her and she closed her eyes, opening them fast when the door slammed shut as Ross strode in. He was blazing with temper and she had never seen his jaw set in such an uncompromising line.

'What a bitch you are! Is this how you got your own back?' he flared.

'My own back? I don't follow.'

'The note you wrote Gary Winton, telling him to ask me those questions.' He came menacingly towards her, and she stepped back, frightened he was going to strike her. 'I know you despise me, but I didn't think you'd allow it to jeopardise our business relationship.'

'What note?' Abby cried.

'Don't play dumb! Lying won't help.'

'I'm not lying. I specifically asked Gary *not* to ask you any personal questions,' she defended angrily.

'So why did you write informing him he was at liberty to ask anything he wanted?' Ross flung her a fulminating look. 'He gave it me to read.'

'Impossible. I tell you I haven't written to him!'

'For God's sake stop lying!' Ross shouted the words, and then with an enormous effort, controlled himself. 'It was typed on your company paper and signed by you. I'm sorry I disappointed you by not making a fool of myself. Then you'd really have had something to gloat over. You have a sick mind, Abby, and we're finished. Forget our contract. I don't care if it costs us a packet to get out of it, as long as I won't have to see you again.'

'Acting judge and jury as usual?' she flung at him.

'I'd say it was the pot calling the kettle black,' he grated, and not giving her a chance to reply, stormed out.

Abby stood rooted to the floor. At last she understood the comment Gary had made earlier about getting a more interesting interview. Someone had written to him in her name giving him permission to ask Ross personal questions. But who disliked her so much to stoop so low?

Elize, of course. The girl must have known Ross wanted to play around with her, and had wanted to put a spoke in the wheel. Knowing his aversion to personal publicity, writing to Gary had been the perfect way of doing it. Copying her signature was no problem—Elize could easily have taken a letter she had written to Enrico—but how had she got hold of Stewart and Stewart's headed notepaper?

She remembered the day the girl had called at the office, ostensibly to discuss the interview she was going to do for a woman's chat show, and also to make sure Abby knew that Ross was not free. But there had been a third reason too: to steal a sheet of headed paper.

Yet knowing something and proving it were two different things, but she was determined to clear her name; not simply to make Ross eat his words, but because it impugned her professional integrity.

On tenterhooks she waited for Gary to appear in the hospitality room, and the instant he did, she drew him aside and bluntly informed him she had not sent him the letter he had purportedly received from her.

'So who did?' he asked, intrigued. 'And why?'

'Beats me,' she lied. 'If I saw it, it might help.'

Unfortunately, real-life crime was not like its fiction counterpart, and there were no broken typewriter keys or inky fingerprints to point a guilty finger at the perpetrator. Yet there was positive proof her signature was forged, for close inspection showed it was traced on to the paper in pencil and over-written with a Biro.

'May I keep this?' she asked.

He nodded. 'If you find out who sent it, maybe I can interview them!'

By the time Abby returned home, her pleasure at being able to prove her innocence had faded. There was no point to it. An apology from Ross for wrongly accusing her wasn't going to change anything between them. Elize obviously had a special place in his life, and any other woman was only a passing fancy. Even if he decided to continue with their contract, things had gone too far for her to work amicably with him again.

It was best to cut her losses.

CHAPTER FOURTEEN

AFTER considerable thought, Abby told her parents and cousin about the forged letter, and they agreed it would serve no purpose to show it to Ross, for unless she had firm proof that Elize was behind it, he was more than likely to assume she was trying to smear the girl out of spite.

'Forget the whole thing,' her mother advised. 'Mr Hunt's cancelled the contract and he's out of your life, so concentrate on getting new business.'

If only it were that easy.

Indeed it was made more difficult by her father, who insisted she handle the public relations exercise she had set up prior to her last fearsome row with Ross.

'Why can't *you* do it, Dad?'

'Because you are the one who's handled the Coopers' account, and it's up to you to finish it.'

'I don't see why,' she said obstinately. 'Contractually, we're under no obligation to do any more for them.'

'Don't be silly, my dear. They've paid us in full—which they needn't have done—and they're entitled to have the loose ends tidied up. You were clever enough to persuade TV East to film a fashion show in their Oxford Street branch, and the least you can do is be there to ensure it goes smoothly. Apart from which, we *do* represent other clients, and TV East is an excellent outlet for them too.'

The reasoning was too sound for Abby to argue.

'If you're worried you might see Ross, he won't be there,' her father added. 'Henry Smallwood has agreed to represent the management.'

In spite of it being her last promotion for Coopers', Abby's natural inclination to do her best did not waver, and she decided it would be an excellent selling point to let Coopers' staff model their range of new clothes. After all, very few men or women had the perfect proportions of professionals, and to see clothes looking equally good on less than faultless figures would be a great inducement to shopping there.

To this end, she spent two full days selecting suitable people, and plumped for a variety of ages—in line with the variety of their customers. She also determined to wear something herself from Coopers', and went to their Kensington branch.

Walking through the various departments, she was reminded of her last visit, and her thoughts turned naturally to Caroline, who had accompanied her on that occasion. Her cousin had now completely recovered from her accident, and though still living with Abby's parents, was also in touch with Kevin. Yet he never took her out or came to see her, and when Abby had mentioned it, Caroline had shrugged it off.

'He's terribly busy giving seminars to management trainees.'

'At weekends too? Seems to me he's stringing you along and will let you down again.'

'No, he won't.'

Abby found it hard to credit, but realising Caroline did not wish to admit her affair with him was going nowhere, she had dropped the subject.

'Kevin says Ross is dating lots of different women,' her cousin had confounded her by saying. 'It seems to me he isn't as committed to marrying Elize as she'd like you to believe.'

'I don't see it that way. She's kept him waiting three years and he's probably showing her he's losing patience.'

'Then now is your chance to get back in his life.'

'No, thanks,' Abby had retorted. 'The pocket Venus won't let him go that easily. Now let's talk about someone nice—like Charlie!'

Abby was a bundle of nerves the day of the shoot, and took longer than usual to get ready. Staring at her reflection in one of the mirrored wardrobes ranged along one wall of her bedroom, she admired the outfit she had bought. High fashion mixed with timeless classic in the coffee and cream double breasted wool jacket, short skirt, and cream silk shirt. Copied from a Paris model, it had cost a twentieth of the price, and was good enough to fool all but the most discerning eye, as were the shoes and bag in beige leather, with Chanel-style gold trim. Much as she disliked Elize, she had to admit the girl was one of the best fashion buyers in the industry.

Because she had been sleeping badly for weeks, Abby was unusually pale, and to bring life to her skin she was heavy with her foundation and blusher. Happily, her hair had not lost its natural sheen and bounce, and required little attention. Allowing a few red-gold fronds to curl on her temples, she swept the rest away from her face, which drew attention to the slender curve of her neck, and the charmingly tilted nose.

Efficient, but feminine with it, she concluded, grabbing her briefcase and hurrying out to the taxi she had ordered.

Arriving at the Oxford Street branch, she found TV East vans parked at the side-entrance, and their technicians installing their lighting in the clothes department on the first floor.

'If the models look half as great in the clothes as you do,' Lance Evans, producer of the show, commented, coming over to greet her, 'you'll have customers queuing in the aisles!'

'They already do,' she grinned, aware of Marissa Brown, who was going to write the commentary, hovering at her elbow.

Mr Newman, the manager of the store, joined them. 'Sorry I can't welcome you in my office, but it's being refurbished, and isn't the most comfortable place to sit in.'

After coffee was served and drunk, they were taken around the various departments to see the latest innovations, and hear of those planned. Normally Abby would have enjoyed herself, but knowing she had no role to play in Coopers' future spoiled her interest. Added to this was the niggling fear Ross might appear. It would be like him to turn up when he was least expected.

'Ah, Miss Stewart.' The grey-headed figure of Henry Smallwood bore down on her. 'Lovely to see you again. Still keeping up the good work, eh?'

Responding to his greeting, it occurred to her he might be unaware of their cancelled contract, and she decided to say nothing about it. He would want to know why, and since he was no longer concerned with the running of the company there was no point discussing it.

'I hope Rossiter won't eradicate Smallwood's image completely,' he confided in her. 'Our style of trading was a little old-fashioned, I grant you, but our customers were loyal to us because they liked things that way.'

Unfortunately not sufficient had done so, Abby thought, otherwise he would not have had to merge with Coopers'.

'I don't think you need worry,' she assured him. 'Mr Hunt is doing all he can to retain your caring image.'

'I'm so glad,' Henry Smallwood said approvingly. 'I'd like to have a little talk with you. When you can get away, perhaps we can meet in Mr Newman's office.'

'Give me thirty minutes,' she replied.

It was closer to an hour before she managed to extricate herself from the mêlée that invariably occurred during filming, and take the escalator to the second floor.

She was curious why Mr Smallwood wanted to talk to her privately, and wondered if she was wrong in thinking he didn't know their contract had been terminated. If so, he might offer to act as an intermediary to resolve their differences. After all, he had always been keener than Ross to employ them.

Surprisingly, there was no sign of him in the manager's office, nor of any workmen either. They had probably gone to lunch, she decided after consulting her watch and seeing it was half-past twelve. Paint, rolls of paper, and other building material lay about the room, and the nearest thing to seating was a ladder.

Bored, she perched on a lower rung and stared out of the dusty window at the teeming crowds below in Oxford Street. How long should she wait for Mr Smallwood? she wondered when ten minutes had elapsed, and had risen to go in search of him when the door behind her opened.

With a smile she turned, but instead of the elderly chairman, a scruffily dressed man in his forties, with an unshaven face and lank fair hair, entered the room and locked the door behind him.

'What are you doing?' Abby demanded, half rising.

'Sit down and be quiet,' he ordered.

Abby's heart drummed a tattoo, and she looked wildly at the telephone lying on the floor within arm's reach. But he caught her glance.

'Don't try anything foolish,' he warned, his voice rough but not uneducated, 'or I'll explode this.'

With a gasp of horror she saw he was holding a hand grenade, and though she wasn't certain if it was real she knew it would be stupid to assume it wasn't.

'If I pull out the pin,' he added conversationally, 'this whole section will blow sky high—with *you* inside it.'

With you too, she thought desperately, but icy fear stopped her from provoking him. Was he a madman? Why else was he keeping her prisoner? Panic set her heart racing, and perspiration trickled between her breasts.

'W-why are you—what do you want? If it's money——'

'Right. But not yours,' he cut in impatiently. 'You weren't supposed to be here. It was the old guy I wanted. But when the workmen left for lunch, and I had the chance of catching him alone, he suddenly left the room. I hung around waiting for him to come back, but he didn't. Then you came in and I had to take second best.' He stared nervously at the door. 'My wife worked here for three years, but when the second lot of twins were born and she took two years off, they refused to take her back.'

'That's understandable,' Abby said, instantly regretting her remark when he snarled at her.

'Understandable that we should starve? I wrote and told the bastards I'd had a breakdown and couldn't work, but they still wouldn't change their minds.'

'How can holding me help you? I'm just a customer who wandered in here by mistake,' Abby said desperately.

'Shut your lying mouth! I've watched Coopers' headquarters for months, and seen you come and go, so I know you're connected with them.'

Abby had assumed his action was spur-of-the-moment, and hearing he had planned it made her position seem far more dangerous. From what she had read of similar situations, her best course of action was to be sympathetic to his cause and keep him talking, in the hope he would eventually regard her as a friend, and think twice before harming her.

'Why did you want to capture Mr Smallwood?' she questioned, drawing on all her reserves of strength to keep her tone friendly and casual.

'He was the easiest one to get. I'd have preferred Hunt, but men like him have twenty-four-hour protection.'

Abby took mental note of this. Her kidnapper, for all his talk, wasn't as *au fait* with company matters as he pretended.

'How much do you want?' she asked.

'Two hundred thousand pounds in cash, and safe conduct for my wife and kids to Spain. When she phones to tell me she's arrived, I'll let you go.'

Abby hid her dismay at hearing such a ridiculous plan. Even if his wife was given the money and left the country, he himself had no hope of escaping. He was definitely mad.

'Where's your wife now?' she asked.

'In fifteen minutes she'll be in a taxi with the kids, outside the front entrance. Packed and ready to go to Spain. I told her I have a job there.'

'You've worked it out very well.'

'When you're on the dole, you have plenty of time to plan.'

'I understand.'

'Like hell you do!' he snarled. 'Now pick up the phone and call Hunt. Say Eric Ramsey's holding you hostage, and what my terms are for releasing you.'

With shaking hands Abby dialled Ross's private office line, offering a silent prayer of thanks when he answered it. Heaven knew what Ramsey would have done had there been no reply.

'H-hello, Ross,' she stammered. 'It's Abby.'

'What do you want?' His voice was brusque.

What did he suppose she wanted? To kiss and make up? Battening down her hysteria, she said shakily, 'I'm being held hostage by a Mr Eric Ramsey, in the manager's office of your Oxford Street store.'

'*You're what*?'

'Listen carefully, Ross,' she continued, and relayed the exact instructions her kidnapper had given her.

Stunned silence was her answer, and it was clear Ross was having difficulty believing what she had said.

'Has he harmed you? Are you all right?' he finally enquired, all brusqueness gone from his voice.

'I'm fine. But—but Mr Ramsey is holding a hand grenade.'

The silence this time was longer. 'Are you sure it's real?' came the quiet question.

'Tell him I'll pull the pin,' Eric Ramsey said beside her, almost as if he had divined the question. 'Doesn't matter to me if I die, but I'll take you with me.'

The sharp expletive resounding in Abby's ear told her Ross had heard the remark.

'Keep calm and be nice to him,' he said in a whisper. 'I'll get back to you soon.'

The phone clicked off, and so did the voice of sanity, leaving her overwhelmed with panic. Suppose her captor realised Ross had no intention of complying with his demands? His nervous pacing told her he was psyched up enough to do anything. Was he high on drugs too? His eyes were glazed, with dark, bruise-like patches beneath, but that could be due to tightly strung nerves.

'I won't wait long,' he snapped. 'I'm not asking for a fortune. He probably earns more for himself in a year. If he tries to play funny...'

The grenade shook in his hand, and Abby's heart seemed to turn in her breast. She wanted to pacify him but couldn't think what to say, and was searching for the right words when the telephone rang.

'No tricks,' he warned as she went to answer it. 'You inform Mr Bloody Hunt that if he plays me for a fool, I'll pull the pin.'

'Abby?' Ross's voice was calm and very quiet. 'Can Ramsey hear me?'

'No, I'm fine,' she said. 'Just fine.'

'Good. Now listen carefully. I've notified the police, and everyone else in the store. But make him believe I'll do exactly as he's asked, but that I don't have such a large sum of money available and have to collect it from the bank.'

'What's the bastard saying?' Ramsey demanded. 'I told you not to talk long.'

'He has to get the money from the bank.'

'When will it be here?' Before she could answer, the man snatched the receiver from her hand and shouted into it. 'Listen to me, Mr Bloody Hunt, I want the money pronto. And charter a plane to take my family to Malaga the minute my wife gets the money. The quicker she gets there, the sooner your girlfriend will be free.'

The receiver slammed back on its rest and Abby felt totally isolated, as if she and her kidnapper were the only two people left in the entire world. No sound reached them, save the dimmed noise of traffic beyond the closed window. She looked at the door and frowned. Ross had said he had notified everyone what was going on, and she half expected to hear some sounds from outside the room.

'I locked the doors the other side of the corridor too,' Eric Ramsey said, intercepting her glance. 'So don't look for any rescue attempt. And if they try...' He shook his fist with the grenade clutched in it. 'Where's the damned money? What are they doing—printing it?'

'It's not easy to raise so much,' Abby reiterated soothingly. 'Mr Hunt is doing everything he can.'

'You in love with him?' Eric Ramsey enquired suddenly.

'Of course not.'

The man's lips curled in a sneer. 'Then why did you go to bed with him? And don't bother shaking your head and lying, because I followed you the day he took you to the river, and he didn't leave your apartment till the early hours of the morning. I bet you weren't talking business—monkey business more like it!'

Abby's skin crawled at the thought of being watched by this man. 'What did you hope to gain by following us?'

'I thought I'd get a chance to snatch him. But then I figured it would be letting him off too easy and he should sweat a little—that they should all sweat a little,' he amended with relish.

'All?' she echoed, puzzled. 'I don't understand.'

'His friends and family,' Eric Ramsey explained. 'I found out who they were by following him, and then threatened them too, so he had no way of guessing who my target was going to be.'

Abby tried to make some sense of what he was saying, but was in no state to reason clearly. The minutes dragged, and she began to despair. Her captor too became restless, pacing the floor like a caged animal.

Suddenly a deep, muffled voice from the street penetrated the room, calling to them to open the window.

'You open it,' Ramsey barked at her. 'I'm no sucker to be used for target practice.'

The double-glazed window frame was stiff and heavy and Abby struggled to lift it. It gave abruptly, and as she leaned out, her captor pulled her roughly back inside, but not before she had managed to glimpse police cars with a throng of men around them.

'Eric Ramsey?' Ross's voice boomed through a loud-speaker, and recognising it, Abby almost cried with joy.

'Eric Ramsey,' he repeated, 'I am Rossiter Hunt, and I have just handed two hundred thousand pounds to your wife. She's here and wants to speak to you.'

The man took Abby's place at the window, but held her in front of him as a shield as his wife confirmed what Ross had said. She then went on to assure him she and the children were being taken to Luton Airport to fly to Malaga on a private jet Ross had ordered, and promised to telephone him the instant she arrived there.

A slight shadow fell across the corner of the window and Abby held her breath. Someone was there. If Eric Ramsey saw him, he would go berserk. With a loud moan she sagged against him, as if she had fainted, and he fell back as all her weight slumped on him.

'What the hell are you doing?' he shouted.

'Sorry,' she gasped, the rough material of his jacket rasping her face as she burrowed her head into him, pushing him even further back into the room. 'I feel ill.'

'Then lie on the floor.'

He pushed her away and she pretended to stagger, managing to edge nearer to the window. As she did, she glimpsed a man on the ledge, carrying what appeared to be a hose.

A muffled thud from somewhere in the building had Eric Ramsey spinning round with alarm, and Abby was positive an attempt would be made to get to them from within the store, as well as from outside.

She started talking, hoping to distract her kidnapper from any other intrusive sounds that might arise. But he would have none of it.

'Shut your mouth,' he shouted, 'or I'll do it for you! If those bastards try to rush in here I'll—— Urgh!'

His ranting was cut short by a high-powered jet of water wooshing through the window and knocking him on to the floor, while simultaneously the door crashed open and two burly policemen catapulted into the room and overpowered him.

But it was the sight of Ross, tie askew, face grey with anxiety, that brought home to Abby the danger she had been in. Her relief was so great that she began trembling, agitated movements that shook her entire body. The room receded, growing darker and smaller.

'Ross!' she cried, then knew no more.

CHAPTER FIFTEEN

'ABBY, darling, you're safe, it's all over.'

Her father's voice came to her as though through a blanket of cotton wool, and her lids fluttered open to see him crouched down next to her, behind him a younger, broader figure, equal concern in the grey eyes set beneath well-shaped chestnut eyebrows.

'Daddy...Ross,' she whispered, momentarily wondering where she was. Then recollection made her try to lift her head from the makeshift pillow on which she lay on the floor, but the room blurred and she fell back again. 'I feel so giddy.'

'It's shock; you'll be fine soon,' her father said, getting to his feet. 'I'll call your mother and let her know you're all right.'

'How did you know I was——?'

'Ross telephoned and I dashed straight here.'

As he went from the room, Abby's eyes moved to the younger man. 'What's happened to Eric Ramsey?'

'The police have taken him away.'

'He's not wicked, Ross. He had a breakdown and he lost his job and couldn't cope. I'm sure he wouldn't have pulled the pin on the grenade.'

'I wouldn't bet my last fiver on it!' came the dry response.

He straightened, seeming to tower above her. Yet he did not exude his usual air of confidence, and she noticed how pale and tired he was, with lines cutting grooves either side of his mouth, and puffiness under his eyes.

'You look the way I feel,' she said candidly.

'I was worried about you.'

'That made two of us,' she joked, refusing to read anything other than normal concern in his statement.

Before he could say more, her father reappeared, Henry Smallwood with him.

'My dear young lady, what a fright you gave us! If only I'd waited for you, Ramsey would have taken *me* hostage and you wouldn't have had to go through such an ordeal. But when you didn't arrive, I assumed you were too busy, and went off to lunch.'

'Don't blame yourself,' she said quickly. 'It's all over and I'm fine.'

'Thanks to Ross,' Mr Stewart added. 'If he'd allowed the police to storm the room, as they wanted, lord knows what that man would have done.'

Abby's love for Ross washed over her with renewed force, and she would have given anything to have him hold her. Well, almost anything. What she couldn't give was the discarding of her moral stance; her belief that you didn't go to bed with one girl when you were involved with another.

'I'm very grateful,' she murmured, forcing herself to meet his gaze.

He shrugged. 'You're making me sound the hero of the hour when it should be you.'

'There are reporters and a television crew outside clamouring to come in and interview you both,' Mr Stewart interjected.

'I don't want to see anyone,' Abby said shakily, and Henry Smallwood patted her shoulder reassuringly.

'You take it easy and rest. I'll have a word with them myself.'

He hurried out, and Mr Stewart, ever the public relations consultant, went with him.

'How did the media get to hear of this?' Abby asked Ross.

'Someone tipped them off.'

'*You*?'

'Why the hell should I have called the papers?'

'Because my kidnapping was great free publicity for Coopers'!'

His face darkened angrily. 'That kind of cheap stunt is more your line.'

'Thanks—I think the world of you too!'

Expecting a sarcastic riposte, she was astonished by his look of contrition.

'Forgive me, Abby. My nerves are shot to pieces, and if——' He broke off as her father returned.

'You *should* talk to the press and TV, my dear. If you don't, they'll keep hounding you.'

'I hate it when you're right!' Woozily she sat up, growing even woozier at the touch of Ross's hands as he helped her to her feet.

'Hey—don't go fainting on me,' he warned with mock severity.

'I'm more shaken than I thought,' she lied. 'I'll be OK in a minute. How do I look?'

'Pale and very interesting!'

Once on her feet, her normal resilience returned, and with Ross and her father either side of her, she went down to face the media.

Their questions came thick and fast, and when she had answered them, they turned their interest on Ross.

'Is it true that not only you, but your friends and business associates also received threatening phone calls from Eric Ramsey?'

'Yes.'

'What did you do?'

'Refused to be blackmailed, and consulted with the police. At noon today they gave me a list of suspects, and Ramsey topped the list. They were on their way to pick him up when Miss Stewart called me to say he had taken her hostage.'

Abby began to wilt, and noticing it, Ross placed a protective arm around her shoulders. 'Please excuse us, gentlemen. As you see, Miss Stewart is exhausted and anxious to return to her home.' Without further ado, he ushered her to his car.

'Your mother wants you to stay with us for a few days,' Mr Stewart said, materialising beside them. 'And no argument.'

'Who's arguing?'

Smiling at her unexpected submission, her father went to hail a cab, but Ross wouldn't hear of it and insisted on driving them.

Abby sat in the back and listened to the two men discussing the whole sorry story.

'At first I assumed his threats were a hoax,' Ross said. 'But when people close to me also started receiving them, I began to take it seriously.'

'You've had a worrying few months.'

'You can say that again! And made even worse by having to carry on as if everything was normal.'

'A lesser man would have buckled under the strain.'

Abby was annoyed by the way Ross had ingratiated himself into her father's good books. While she appreciated he was grateful to Ross for the part he had played in her rescue, she wished he would remember that this selfsame man refused to believe that the letter to Gary Winton had been a cruel hoax at her expense, to say nothing of the way he had pressured Kevin into breaking with Caroline.

So irritated was she that next morning, when a lavish basket of roses arrived for her from Ross, she instantly ordered a cab to take it to the children's ward of the local hospital.

'I know you've had your disagreements,' her mother protested, 'but given that you probably owe your life to him, can't you forgive and forget?'

'No.'

'He'd like to talk to you. He telephoned when you were asleep and I said you'd ring him.'

'Well, I won't; and if you keep nagging me about him, I'll go back to my apartment.'

It was a threat guaranteed to silence her mother, though it made Abby hate herself and, alone in her bedroom, she gave way to tears.

'It's reaction from shock,' her mother commented, coming back into the room with a cup of hot chocolate and some shortcake. 'Get this inside you and have another sleep.'

'You shouldn't spoil me like this,' she protested.

'In lieu of grandchildren, what else can I do?'

Biting back a sigh, Abby sipped her chocolate.

'Caroline says to tell you she's sorry she didn't come in to see you before she left for work,' Mrs Stewart went on, 'but she'll try to leave the office early.'

Curious to know if Kevin had also been a recipient of Eric Ramsey's threats, Abby was tempted to call her cousin, but in the end decided to wait until she saw her this evening. She had not felt like discussing it last night, for all she had wanted was to sleep.

Six o'clock came and went without any sign of Caroline, and she was still not home when they went in to dinner.

'She's never been this late.' Mrs Stewart glanced worriedly at her husband. 'She always makes sure she's back in time to play with Charlie before he goes to bed.'

'I haven't seen her all day,' he replied, looking equally concerned. 'I was out of the office seeing clients.'

'I'll call my secretary,' Abby volunteered, pushing back her chair. 'They share an office and Sandy may know where she is.'

Abby was halfway across the room when Caroline burst in, her face ashen.

'I'm a widow!' she cried. 'Jeffrey was killed this afternoon in a motor accident.'

Everyone stared at her, too shocked to speak.

'He was drunk,' she went on, her voice shrill with distress.

'Who told you?' Abby questioned.

'His sister. Apparently he crashed into a wall in the early hours of this morning.'

'Come and sit down and I'll get you a drink,' Mr Stewart intervened. 'Whisky or brandy?'

'Neither, thanks. I'm going to my room if you don't mind. I'd like to be alone.'

She went out, and Abby looked at her parents. 'How can she be so upset? Jeffrey was an absolute swine to her and the baby.'

'She's crying for the might-have-been,' Mrs Stewart sighed, 'not for what was.'

Abby, all too aware she had done the same over Ross, was instantly silenced, realising her mother's comments could equally apply to herself.

It was in a muted frame of mind that she retired to her room, and she was already in bed when her cousin knocked on the door and came in. Her skin was blotchy and her eyes red, but she was otherwise composed.

'I never imagined I'd shed any tears over Jeffrey, but his death really shook me.'

'It's only natural,' Abby sympathised and, patting the side of the bed for Caroline to sit down, listened in silence as she went over the old ground of her marriage to

Jeffrey, seeing it as the therapy she needed to expunge any feelings of guilt over his death.

'I rang Kevin and told him,' she concluded, 'and he said I should move in with him right away.'

'You're a sucker for punishment,' Abby expostulated. 'What if he changes his mind again, the way he did last time?'

'He didn't change it.' Caroline went pink with embarrassment. 'I wanted to tell you this yesterday, but you were so traumatised, I left it. You see, the only reason he acted as he did was that the very morning I was going to move in, *he* got a threatening call too, and when he told Ross, Ross said it would be safer for me if I stayed away from Kevin till the blackmailer was caught.'

Abby was dumbstruck, then filled with remorse as she recollected the accusations she had flung at Ross; only now did she realise how unjust they had been. But why hadn't he apprised her of the truth?

'Did Kevin tell you this last night?'

'No.' Caroline went pinker. 'In the hospital.'

'And you never let on, even when I blamed Ross for it?'

'Kevin swore me to secrecy. Ross was afraid that if too many people knew what was going on, someone would start looking over their shoulder, and alert the blackmailer that he had gone to the police.'

'At least it explains why you didn't bear a grudge against Kevin,' Abby sighed. 'But it means me eating humble pie with Ross.'

'I know, and I'm truly upset. But quite honestly, it was up to him to put you in the picture.'

'You're dead right,' Abby said, the bitterness of rejection souring her voice. Ross had not told her what was going on because he hadn't cared whether or not she thought badly of him. 'I don't think I'll eat humble pie after all,' she said, giving an ostentatious yawn to show she was tired.

Taking the hint, her cousin leaned forward to kiss her goodnight. 'Maybe he didn't tell you because he didn't want to worry you?'

'Forget it. It's water under the bridge.' Abby faked another yawn. 'Turn off the main light on your way out, will you, honey? I'm too tired to read.'

Caroline did as asked, and the moment the door closed behind her Abby buried her head under the pillow and burst into tears.

Next day she moved back to her apartment, and in the afternoon resumed work, knowing that to stay home moping would not help her get over Ross; and get over him she must.

With demonic energy she flung herself into a new campaign for one of their clients, and though she was soon her normal self outwardly, the effort to appear carefree took its toll of her, and she grew physically thinner and brittle in manner.

'You look as if a puff of wind will blow you away,' her father observed late one afternoon, when he came in to say goodnight to her.

'Hard work and hard play,' she joked. 'I've a new boyfriend.'

'Several, I believe. Unusual for you, isn't it?'

'I'm changing my image.'

'Or trying to forget Ross.'

'You're right about that. He accused me of being a cheat and a liar, cancelled his contract with us, and——'

'That isn't what I meant, and you know it,' her father interrupted. 'But if you want to keep up the act with me...'

Contrite, Abby reached out and squeezed his hand. 'I'm not shutting you out, Dad. But this is my way of coping with—with things.'

'Fair enough. But remember, bottling up one's emotions isn't always the best way. If ever you——' He stopped as there was a knock at the door and Caroline ran in.

'Oops,' she apologised, glancing from her uncle to Abby. 'I thought you were alone. I'll come back later.'

'I'm going,' Mr Stewart said. 'See you at dinner, Caroline.'

She shook her head. 'I'm moving in with Kevin on Saturday, and we're having dinner tonight with Ross to talk about our wedding. He's offered us his apartment for the reception.'

'I thought you'd be married from our house,' her uncle commented.

'I was when I married Jeffrey, and I'm superstitious about repeating it. You won't mind, will you?'

'Of course not. I'm happy to give you away any place, any time!' Chuckling at his joke, he left the two girls together.

Caroline leaned against the side of the desk and sighed happily. 'I can't believe everything has turned out so marvellously for me. When Jeffrey left me I believed my life was over.'

'Shows what a lousy clairvoyant you'd make!'

'For myself, yes. But not when it comes to *you*. When are you going to admit you love Ross, and put up a fight for him?'

'I'd never fight for a man.' Leaning back in her chair, Abby was the epitome of a relaxed young woman without a care in the world. 'If a man didn't know he loved me, I'd leave him to his ignorance! And just to put the record straight, I do not love Ross. I was attracted to him and hoped something might develop. But it didn't, and I no longer feel anything for him.'

To her own ears she sounded so convincing that she wasn't surprised when Caroline accepted it as the truth, and in the weeks that followed she was forced to grin and bear it when her cousin talked endlessly of Ross, who appeared to be organising the wedding with the same attention to detail he gave to opening a new store!

Intent on showing her family she was carefree and happy, she led a hectic social life that inevitably brought a new man into her orbit.

Andy Preston was the antithesis of Ross, which was probably the reason she began seeing him. A doctor in a successful group practice in Islington, he was average in height, with craggy features, fair hair, and a placid, easygoing temperament. He enjoyed Abby's vivacity and turn of mind, laughed at her anecdotes, teased her about her 'with it' clothes—he was happiest in trousers and sweater—and agreed with her politics. All in all they had everything going for them, as her friends and family pointed out. Except for one thing, Abby knew: she did not love him.

But oh, how she tried. Never had she flung herself into a relationship as whole-heartedly as she did this one, but to no avail. Every time he kissed her she yearned for Ross's mouth, every time he held her, she ached for Ross's arms, and the idea of making intimate love with any man other than Ross was a complete non starter.

Finally she bid Andy goodbye. He wanted more from her than she was ready to give, and it wasn't fair to him to pretend otherwise.

'Is it just me you don't fancy,' he asked, gently rubbing the side of her cheek, 'or are you in love with someone else?'

'You're a lovely, lovely man,' she said, close to tears, 'but we met at the wrong time. I *was* in love with someone and I'm not quite over him.'

'All the more reason to continue seeing me. You know the old adage—the hair of the dog!'

'He's a dog all right!'

'Then it shouldn't be too hard to write him off. I'm willing to see you on a friendship only basis. No pressure, no hassle.'

She was tempted to agree, but was conscious she was far from over Ross; it wasn't fair to give Andy hope.

'May we leave it for a while, Andy?'

'If it's what you want. But you know my number, and I hope you won't hesitate to use it.'

Watching him go, she wondered for the hundredth time why one man set your pulses racing and another could leave them flat. If she knew the answer, she could publish it and make a fortune!

CHAPTER SIXTEEN

'You look absolutely stunning,' Abby told Caroline with something approaching relief, as her cousin emerged from one of Chanel's fitting rooms. For the past two days they had scoured Knightsbridge and Bond Street for an outfit for her to wear at her wedding, and had finally found one.

'It's certainly the nicest suit I've seen,' Caroline agreed, 'but it costs an arm and a leg.'

'Kevin can afford it, and you're well within the budget he's allowed you.'

'I know. "Budget" has a whole new connotation since I've been living with him! In the past I always associated it with scrimping and scraping.'

'Will *madame* take the suit with her or shall we deliver it?' the saleswoman enquired.

'Deliver it, please,' Caroline said in her poshest voice, giving her cousin a wink as she did. 'We're lunching at Claridge's.'

'Since when?' Abby asked as they stepped into the street.

'Since you reminded me I no longer have to scrimp and save!'

Crossing Bond Street, they walked the short distance to the hotel, but did not speak of intimacies until they were seated at a table in the Causerie, where they could enjoy one of the best buffet lunches in London.

'I can't believe the wedding is only a couple of weeks away!' Caroline exclaimed. 'The last few months have been the happiest of my life. I just wish things were going well for *you*.'

'I've no complaints. I have two new clients who are happy to agree with any promotions I suggest, and I'm thoroughly enjoying the art class I've joined. In fact I'm considering going two evenings a week instead of one.'

'Is that the extent of your social life—art classes? Honestly, Abby, who do you think you're fooling? It's obvious you haven't got over Ross, and——'

'You're not still on *that* track, are you?'

'Yes, I am.'

'Then get off it! He's managing very well without me, and I'm doing the same without him.'

'I suppose you read that piece in Edwin Baker's column?' Caroline referred to a well-known gossip columnist.

'And others.'

'So what if he's dating Elize again? She's like part of his family. Anyway, he's seeing other girls too.'

'Particularly a luscious French actress.'

'I'm sure it doesn't mean anything. Look at all the guff that was printed about you after the kidnapping. Most of it wasn't true, and the same thing could apply to that actress and Ross.'

'And the New York writer and Ross, and the blonde model who's just signed up to work for him, and Rosie what's her name whose latest song has been in the top ten for six weeks? Come off it, will you? He's having a whale of a time and I couldn't care less.'

'I give up,' Caroline sighed. 'If you enjoy being alone and miserable, it's your choice.'

'There are *other* men in the world apart from him, you know.'

'Then why aren't you going out with them?'

'If I meet one I like, I will.'

'For a few weeks, maybe, then you'll find an excuse to send him packing—as you did with Andy.'

'Care for another coffee, or shall we get the bill?' Abby questioned.

'All right, I can take a hint! But I'm only saying what your parents and friends are thinking. You can't go on running away from life.'

'One doesn't require a man in it to be fulfilled.'

'*You* do.'

After Abby had dropped off Caroline at Kevin's house, she couldn't help silently acknowledging that her cousin had spoken the truth. She *was* wasting her life, and she *did* need a man in it. But it could never be a two-timing one like Ross. Even now, knowing he had gone from her bed to Elize's filled her with bitter shame, to say nothing of the accusations he had flung at her the night he had appeared on the Gary Winton show. But how to get over him? A frenzy of work had not helped, nor had dating other men. It seemed as though she'd have to rely on the old adage of time being the great healer.

But next morning, Ross was brought vividly to mind when she received a telephone call from Eric Ramsey's wife.

'I hope you don't mind my calling you?' the woman began in a soft, nervous voice. 'But I saw Mr Hunt yesterday, and though he said you'd recovered from—from your ordeal, I felt I had to talk to you myself. I feel so guilty that——'

'You shouldn't. It wasn't your fault.'

'Yes, it was. I should have realised how ill my husband was and insisted he saw a doctor. But I was too busy nursing my grievances against Coopers' to realise that he was suffering too. Eric isn't a wicked man, Miss Stewart. He'd never have used that hand grenade. But he was desperate and sick, and——'

'Please don't upset yourself,' Abby interrupted. 'I've put it behind me and I'm fine.' But how was this poor woman coping? she thought, and was wondering how to phrase the question when it was answered for her.

'Eric's in a mental hospital, you know, and Mr Hunt's making sure he gets the best possible treatment. He's a marvellous man, Miss Stewart. He found me a job with a friend of his, and he's paid all our debts; but I'm sure you know this, or I wouldn't be telling you. That's the one thing he insisted on—that I kept it secret.'

Long after the call had ended, Abby pondered on it. She wished she could say she was surprised by Ross's caring behaviour, but she couldn't; it was exactly what she would have expected of him. It was only in his personal life that he had no scruples.

As the day of Caroline's wedding dawned, Abby was a bundle of nerves. With no chance of getting out of it, she had determined to look as stunning as possible, and her jade-green silk suit hugged her body like a second skin, turning her eyes into glittering emeralds, and enhancing the red-gold of her artlessly tousled hair. Ross had once fancied her enough to cheat on Elize, and she intended reminding him of what he was missing!

The marriage was being performed at Marylebone Register Office, and when she arrived with her mother most of the guests were already outside, waiting in glorious, if cool autumn sunshine, for the bride to arrive with her young son and her uncle. Even though Caroline had moved into Kevin's home, in keeping with tradition she had not wanted him to see her in her dress until the ceremony, and had spent the previous night at her aunt and uncle's house.

Unobtrusively Abby searched for Ross, spotting his tall, commanding figure at the back, where he stood with Elize and an older woman who, from the uncanny resemblance, was clearly her mother.

Unexpectedly he turned his head and their eyes met. Briefly he nodded to her, then turned back to Elize, a glowing picture in red. Red again! Recollecting it was the selfsame colour as the dress he had bought Elize during their trip to the Midlands, Abby wondered if he had chosen this one too.

'So that's the competition,' her mother muttered.

'Competition?' Abby repeated with pseudo innocence. 'What are you talking about?'

'Who, my dear, not what! The pretty brunette beside Rossiter Hunt.'

Before her mother could say anything further, the bridal car arrived, and as everyone surged towards it Abby found herself standing next to Ross. The temptation to fling herself into his arms was overwhelming, and she inched back. She had been dreading this encounter and was glad they were amid a crowd, where thoughts could not be easily read and emotions could more easily be hidden.

'Hello,' she smiled, forcing herself to look at him. His eyes were a pale grey this morning, the lashes as thick and dark as she remembered, his mouth as finely cut, his body—damn it, this must stop! 'How are you?' she went on, cool as ice.

'Fine. No need to ask how you are, you look wonderful.'

'Why, thank you, I feel wonderful. How's business?'

'Excellent.'

The calm measuredness of his tone was the very antithesis of her own pent-up emotions, and resentment coursed through her. Thankfully it wasn't necessary to rack her brains for more small talk, for the bridal group were approaching, and Caroline, radiant in sugared almond pink, stopped on the stone steps to give them both a hug.

'Kevin's inside, I take it?' she beamed. 'I'd hate to be left in the lurch!'

'No worry on that score,' Ross grinned. 'He was dressed and ready to leave the house at eight this morning.'

Charlie, adorable in long black velvet trousers and white satin lace-trimmed shirt, tugged at Ross's hand for attention, and the man went down on his haunches and talked to him on his level.

'Hello, young man. Have you come to give your mother away?'

'Uncle Kev,' the little boy answered.

'That's right. You're giving your mother to Uncle Kev, and she's giving you a daddy in return.' Ross drew the child into his arms as if to the manner born, and straightened. 'I'll carry him inside for you,' he informed Caroline. 'It's a long walk for little legs.'

'It's a long walk for *my* legs,' she admitted. 'I'm shaking like a leaf.'

'OK, if you carry your son, *I'll* carry you!'

Laughing, she led the way in, and seeing his mother disappear, Charlie wriggled round in Ross's arms and leaned towards Abby.

'Abba hold,' he ordered, his lower lip trembling, and Abby gathered him close before he burst into tears.

'How maternal you look,' Elize said to her, rejoining Ross and linking her arm through his. 'I hope he won't cry during the ceremony.'

'If he does, I'm sure his mother and Kevin won't mind,' Ross put in before Abby could answer, and deftly propelled Elize into the town hall.

Gratified by his response, Abby searched out her mother among the throng, and joined her.

Happily, Charlie sat quiet as a mouse on Abby's lap, too young at twenty-three months to understand what was going on, but intelligent enough to sense it was an important occasion. But as soon as wedding rings had been exchanged, he jumped off and toddled over to his mother.

'I miss having him around the house,' Mrs Stewart confessed. 'It made me realise why all my friends enjoy being grandparents.'

'If that's a hint...'

'How clever of you to guess!'

Mr Stewart joined them for the drive to the reception, and as they entered Ross's apartment she relived the first occasion she had come here. She had been bowled over by him then, and she was bowled over by him today. It was depressing to know she was no nearer forgetting him, and with an effort she concentrated on the festivities around her.

There were flowers everywhere, and a huge bank of them in the entrance hall, where Caroline, Kevin, his mother and Abby's parents formed a reception line. After watching some of the guests arrive, she wandered on to the terrace, which had been covered by a silk-draped marquee for the occasion. It was soon filled with people, and staff bustled around offering champagne and canapés of smoked salmon and caviare.

Ross had spared no expense to make this a memorable occasion, and she sourly wondered when *he* would get married. The idea of it was enough to make her reach for a glass of champagne. Effervescent, its potency worked quickly, and she joined some friends of hers and Caroline's, laughing and joking as if she did not have a care in the world.

It was only as she caught sight of Ross, circling the room, talking to guests, yet religiously avoiding her, that her spirits drooped. What was there about him that made him so hard for her to forget? She could count on her fingers the number of times she had seen him socially, and they had gone to bed only once; hardly the stuff of which great romances were made. Yet her love for him had blossomed and refused to wilt, no matter how cold the frost of disillusion.

'Don't you agree?' one of her friends asked her, and Abby—who had not heard a word—looked so blank that everyone laughed.

'Too much champagne on an empty stomach,' she excused. 'I'll go stoke up!'

Grateful for an excuse to escape, she headed for the buffet and, soon hidden from sight of her friends, changed direction—eating was abhorrent to her at the moment—and made for the study she had glimpsed on her way into the apartment.

It was octagonal in shape, and dark green and gold in colour, with an exquisite Regency sofa table and deep, comfortable chairs upholstered in ruby-red velvet. With a sigh she collapsed into one of them.

'Tired, or antisocial?' a feminine voice questioned, and Abby swung round to see Elize watching her. Was the girl following her to make sure she didn't speak to Ross alone, or was it coincidence?

'I'm tired,' she replied. 'Caroline and I were up till all hours talking, and it's catching up on me.'

'She's bubbling like champagne.'

'It must be the effervescence of love.'

'What a charming expression.' Elize sank into an easy chair opposite her. 'I'm getting married myself, you know.'

Abby felt as if the air had been squeezed from her lungs. 'Congratulations,' she managed to say. 'Does—does that mean you're leaving Coopers', or have you persuaded Ross to let you stay on?'

'Oh, no, I'm giving it up. We'll be living in Paris.'

'Paris?' Mingled with Abby's amazement was a sense of reprieve; at least she wouldn't be afraid of bumping into them when she visited Caroline.

'Is Ross selling out, or letting someone else become managing director?'

'Neither. He's staying put.' Elize smoothed her immaculate hair. 'I'm not marrying Ross.'

Abby's brain refused to function and she could not speak.

'I'm marrying Jacques Castelle,' Elize went on.

Abby's brain clicked into gear. 'Of Castelle's department stores?'

'The very one. I was nosing round their Paris branch and bumped into this maddeningly bossy man who demanded to know why I was making notes as I walked around. I wouldn't tell him and we had a flaming row. From then on, it was uphill all the way!'

'It must have been a shock for Ross,' Abby murmured.

'Only because I fell in love so unexpectedly. My family and friends have always considered me aloof and controlled, and I thought the same too—until I met Jacques. He made me realise that what I felt for Ross was a schoolgirl crush that I'd refused to let go.' Gracefully Elize rose, went to the door and locked it. 'You and I should have a proper talk.'

'I don't see why.'

'You will in a minute.' Elize resumed her seat. 'Ross and I were close years ago, as you obviously guessed, but our affair had burned itself out long before you came on the scene—or at least it had on his part. But I still hoped to get him back, and while he was playing the field, I felt I had a chance. However once you waltzed into his life it was a different proposition. He went overboard for you.'

'A little flirtation,' Abby shrugged.

'A hell of a lot more! He fell in love with you. That's why he dropped you so suddenly.'

'I don't follow you.'

'Hear me out first. Everyone connected with Ross received threatening calls from Eric Ramsey. Of course at the time we didn't know who it was—just a whispering voice saying we, or people dear to us, would meet with an accident if the money wasn't paid. That's why he stopped Caroline moving in with Kevin, and when she was run over he was scared the blackmailer had done it, and might then try to harm *you*.'

'But she walked into the path of a car. It was her own fault,' Abby protested.

'He wasn't certain, and while there was even the slightest doubt in his mind he didn't want to endanger you.'

'Why didn't he tell me the truth instead of pretending he was going to be too busy?'

'He felt you'd ignore his advice and still insist on being with him. Apparently your reaction wasn't what he'd expected—he let something slip to me—and I deduced the rest and decided to make sure the broken pieces stayed broken.' Elize hesitated, then said quickly, 'That's the reason I wrote that letter to Gary Winton. I wanted Ross to think badly of you.'

'You certainly succeeded.'

'I know, and I can only apologise.'

'Why are you telling me this now?' Abby asked.

'Because I want to put things right.'

'It's too late. If Ross loved me, he wouldn't have believed I'd written that letter to Gary.'

'If you loved Ross,' Elize countered, 'you wouldn't have believed me when I came to your office and said he was waiting for me to make up my mind when I'd marry him. You were as quick to think badly of him as he was of you.'

'Then it's best if we stay apart.'

'What a great idea. Two people, loving each other but doing nothing about it.'

Abby stared down at her hands. 'He hasn't exactly pined for me these past months. I've lost count of the girls he's taken out.'

'Window-dressing,' came the forthright reply. 'Look, if you don't want to believe me that's your prerogative, but if you've any sense you'll go and talk to him.' Elize leaned forward and placed her hand on Abby's arm. 'It wasn't easy for me to admit what I've done, so don't let my efforts go to waste.'

'What if you're wrong and he doesn't love me? He might laugh in my face.'

'Take that chance.'

Abby closed her eyes, the better to collate her feelings, and when she opened them again, Elize had gone. Should she pocket her pride and tell Ross how she felt about him? It was a big decision, and one she seemed incapable of making.

Slowly she returned to the terrace. A self-service buffet had been set up at the far end, and though she wasn't hungry, she helped herself to some lobster and sat down next to her parents. Ross was very much in evidence playing host, moving from one guest to another to enquire if they had everything they needed, though she was all too aware that he still kept his distance from her. Elize had to be wrong!

Toasts were proposed and Kevin made a brief speech of thanks. Then the trio, which had been playing popular classics, broke into dance music and bride and groom took to the floor. They were soon followed by others, and Abby noticed Ross cutting in on Caroline. A moment later, Kevin came over and asked her to dance.

'You've been a marvellous cousin to Caroline,' he said. 'I want to thank you.'

Touched by his remark, her eyes filled with tears, and as she blinked them away, they drew abreast of Caroline and Ross.

'Mind if I cut in?' Ross said suavely, swinging Abby into his arms and dancing off with her.

With an immense effort, she did not tense in his arms, though she could not hide her surprise when he suddenly led her off the floor and pulled her swiftly down a carpeted corridor.

'Where are we going?' she questioned, trying to pull free.

'I want to talk to you.' Opening a door, he pushed her into what was obviously his bedroom. 'We won't be disturbed here.'

Abby found herself staring at a king-size bed, and immediately wondered how many women had shared it with him.

'No one but me has slept in it since I met you,' he stated, divining her thoughts.

Abby's cheeks flamed. 'I couldn't care less.'

'That's a pity. If I believed you'd gone to bed with other men since we'd met, I'd be damned upset.' His eyes moved from her autumn-gold hair to her wide red mouth, barely touched by lipstick yet still sweetly curved, and the large green eyes that watched him warily. 'I'm sorry for misjudging you over the letter. Elize told me she wrote it,' he said quietly. 'I believe she told you too.'

Abby nodded. 'I guessed as much anyway.'

'Why didn't you tell me?'

'I couldn't prove it.'

Ross pressed his fingers to his temples. It was an unusual gesture for him to make, and gave her an indication of the strain he was under. If the last months had dealt unkindly with her, they had done the same with him: his face was thinner, with deep hollows beneath the cheekbones.

'I've been jumping to the wrong conclusions about you from the very beginning,' he said grimly.

'I've misjudged you a few times too!'

'You mean with regard to Caroline?'

She nodded. 'And also Elize and a few others.'

'I never dated any woman more than twice, and I never made love to them, though I have to admit I hoped you'd think otherwise.' One dark eyebrow lifted and his expression was mocking. 'I must say I surprised myself. I hadn't realised I was so old-fashioned, but since falling in love with you I haven't wanted anyone else in my bed.'

He came a step nearer but made no attempt to touch her. It was as though he was saying that he had bared his soul and could go no further. The rest was up to her. If she wanted him, she must make the next move.

With a soft cry, she ran towards him and buried her face against the side of his neck. Only then, close to him, was she fully aware of the strain he had been under. He might appear calm on the surface, but his heart was beating as wildly as hers.

'I love you too,' she whispered, twining her fingers through his hair, and revelling in the silky feel of it. 'I can't bear to think of the months we've wasted.'

'Nor can I.' His arms enveloped her, straining her so close she was frightened her ribs would crack. 'I swear I'll make up to you for all the terrible things I said. Forgive me, darling.' His breath was warm on her cheek, his lips soft against the side of her mouth.

'You must forgive me, too,' she said mistily. 'Our trouble was that we fell in love with each other before we knew each other. That's why we were both so defensive and untrusting.' She pulled back from him slightly. 'What would you have done if Elize hadn't told you the truth today?'

'I was going to talk to you anyway. I've been so damn miserable without you, I couldn't go on any longer.'

'Honestly?'

For answer, he released her and went across to the bureau opposite the bed. Opening the first drawer, he took out a folder and handed it to her. Slowly she extracted two airline tickets and a hotel reservation at the Hotel de Paris in Monte Carlo. They were for three days, commencing Friday; and one ticket and one room was in Ross's name, the other in hers.

'I took a chance,' he said gravely. 'Was I right?'

'Very much so,' she said, and dissolved into tears.

With a murmur of pain, Ross pulled her down on the bed and sat next to her. 'Abby, darling, will you marry me?'

'Even though we don't know each other too well?'

'How better to learn than by sharing our lives?'

How better, indeed! Her answer was in her upturned face and parted lips which he covered with his. Their kiss began gently, but almost at once it was as if they were engulfed by flames, so white hot was their passion, so intense their desire. His hands roamed her body, undoing the buttons of her jacket to caress the creamy swell of her breasts, until she moaned and trembled and fell back upon the pillows, pulling him down with her.

'How soon will you marry me?' he whispered against her breasts.

'How soon can you get a licence?' she responded, stroking his ear and enjoying the shudder that pierced him.

'Would you believe I have one?'

'At this precise moment, Mr Hunt, I'll believe anything you tell me!'

'Then I'm telling you that we shall be married a month from now. I won't sleep easy until you're my wife, and any misunderstandings we have can be resolved in our double bed!'

'Sounds fine to me,' she teased, and wriggled free of him. 'Meanwhile there's a wedding outside and some of your relations and mine will be wondering what we're doing in here.'

'Shall we prove them right?'

Her eyes met his without prevarication. 'Do you want to, Ross?'

'Very much, but I won't. When we next make love, I want to touch every part of you, kiss you from top to toe, enter you and never leave you.' His voice deepened and he drew her into his arms again, his body trembling with the effort of self-control. 'It's only a couple of days till we go to Monte Carlo; will you mind waiting?'

'Only on one condition.'

Puzzled, he lifted his head from her breast and looked at her. 'Which is?'

'That we keep the two airline tickets but cancel one bedroom!'

'I'll be happy to oblige,' he said huskily. 'Always, and any time.'